MAKE MINE MURDER

Returning to New York after serving in the Second World War, Gerry Barnes finds himself under pressure from his girlfriend Paula to marry and settle down. To her dismay, he shows little desire to do either: instead, he sets himself up as a private detective! Paula half-jokingly vows to find him his first client — not realizing it will be herself. For when she returns to her hotel, she finds the body of a dead man sprawled on her bed, the handle of a knife sticking up out of his throat!

ROBERT SIDNEY BOWEN

MAKE MINE MURDER

Complete and Unabridged

LINFORD
Leicester

First published in Great Britain

First Linford Edition
published 2018

A catalogue record for this book is available
from the British Library.

ISBN 978–1–4448–3887–9

Published by
F. A. Thorpe (Publishing)
Anstey, Leicestershire

Set by Words & Graphics Ltd.
Anstey, Leicestershire
Printed and bound in Great Britain by
T. J. International Ltd., Padstow, Cornwall

This book is printed on acid-free paper

1

Paula took a light from mine, blew smoke at me, and slid off the corner of the desk. She made a face over her shoulder and went to the window. I let her go because of the sunlight behind her. I sat and smoked and admired the view. All curves.

'It's downright silly, Gerry!'

'It's swell!' I said. 'Turn a little to the left, will you?'

Instead she turned all the way and came back to my desk. Her beautiful face was deadly earnest and pleading.

'It is!' she insisted. 'I simply cannot understand you. I try, but it's — '

'Silly,' I finished before she could. 'You said that before.'

'Oh, shut up and listen!' she blazed. 'I'm only asking you to help me understand!'

I mashed out my cigarette. 'There's nothing to understand, because it's that simple, Paula,' I told her. 'I've always

1

wanted to be a private detective, so I'm going to be a private detective. There isn't any more. Unquote.'

She stamped her foot, flared her nostrils, and slammed her purse on the desk. 'That's no reason!' she cried. 'And it isn't because you have to earn a living, either. You've more money than any one man should have. And if it's thrills — ! Good God, darling, haven't the last four years been thrilling enough for you?'

I shook my head at that one.

'There's nothing thrilling about war, Paula,' I said, and I meant it. 'It's a dirty, rotten mess. Anybody who tells you different is a liar.'

'You weren't drafted!' she flung at me. 'You enlisted even before Pearl Harbor.'

'Skip it,' I said. 'I'm a civilian now. I like it this way best.'

'But why this crazy detective business?' She got back on the beam again. 'Gerry, you're impossible!'

I grinned, and kissed her fast. 'And you're gorgeous. Do me a favor, hmm?'

'What do you want?'

'A small favor,' I said, straight-faced.

'Go get robbed of your jewels and be my first client.'

She banged the desk with her purse again. 'Nuts to being a first client! I want to be your first wife, you ape!'

'I don't need a wife, honey.'

'Yes you do, too!'

'No I don't!'

Bang went the purse. 'Oh, shut up!'

'And I love you, too, baby.' I grinned. To prove it I started to kiss her, but she wasn't having any this time. That was my cue to stop horsing. 'Look, Paula,' I said, 'a private dick shouldn't have a wife . . . like a sailor shouldn't. Not around enough to make it stick.'

'Nuts!' She tossed that away. 'Dammit, Gerry, with your money you can be anything you want. So why . . . ?'

'Thanks to a rich departed uncle, almost anything,' I stopped her. 'So I'm going to be a detective. A good one . . . I hope. By the way, how do you like the layout here?'

'Very crummy,' she said without looking around. 'When does the blonde with the big bazooms start to work?'

'Redhead,' I corrected, and pointed. 'So get me a client, and you're hired.'

A funny look came into her eyes that I didn't get at all. She went back to the window, then swung around, solemn-eyed. 'Okay. It's a deal . . . I'll get you a client,' she said. Then, adding the catch, 'And if you fail to solve the case, you'll give up this crazy idea?'

I shook my head. 'Nope . . . but you get me a case, and I'll let you help me crack it.'

'Woman Friday, eh?' she sniffed.

'Monday, Tuesday, and all the others,' I assured her. 'Make it a murder case. I'm at my best on murders.'

'Maybe it'll be your own!' she said darkly, and came back to the desk. She picked up one of my brand-new business cards and wrinkled her nose. 'Gerry Barnes, Private Investigator. Horses!'

'Special rates for double killings,' I said. 'Don't forget to mention it.'

She started to tear up my card but changed her mind. Instead, she took several more and stuffed them into her purse. Then she leaned close and looked

4

at me with everything one man could desire. 'And I really can't change your mind, darling?' she said softly.

'No, sweet,' I said. 'Some fellows want a crack at the Senate. Even the White House. Me, I want a crack at this business. Like I told you, since I was this high . . . '

She smiled slowly and sadly, like she really did understand how it was with me. 'Okay, Chief! You've got a fireball working for you. I'll start in the Biltmore cocktail lounge. Maybe Nick or Angelo know somebody who's been murdered recently . . . Is your phone connected?'

'Sure.'

She blew a kiss on the way to the door. 'Then stay put and wait for my ring,' she said. 'I'll get you a murder case even if I have to commit one myself!'

'Great,' I called after her. 'But make it somebody I don't like. Clyde Mather would be good.'

The door had closed on the last, but was reopened fast. 'Sir, you are a louse!' she said. 'You are speaking of the man I shall probably have to marry to save my old age. S'long, heel!'

Paula left, but some of the special perfume she used remained. I sat there enjoying it and slowly working the brain down to brass tacks. For fifteen days, I had been a private detective. I had a license to operate as such. I had a gun permit. I had nice-looking business cards, and letterheads. My office was swell — I'd handed out two thousand furnishing it. My name in gold leaf was on the door, and I had a prominent listing in the building lobby. What I didn't have was a client.

And as I sadly mused on that bleak truth, the office door flew open and in came Miss TNT of the current year, or any other year you could mention. Her name was Rita Rollins, and although she wasn't as beautiful as Paula, she had a figure that was strictly all her own. And a pair of jet-black eyes that could do things to make men jump. Quite often out of windows.

I had met Rita at a cocktail party in '41. At the time, she was doing a torch-song number in a current show. She was fun, and because I like fun, too, we had lots and lots of fun. But she got a little too crazy for me, and in the back of her sleek black-haired head was the idea of marriage. I began to see it in her eyes more and more. Marriage is fun, but not with a fireball like Rita. So, slowly and gracefully, I thought, I pulled away. Maybe my meeting Paula during a leave about then helped me pull away faster.

In one flying leap, Rita was in my arms. 'Gerry, Gerry, darling! This is wonderful. I heard about it, and I just had to come see you. I — '

She broke off short and looked around. And a thousand nice memories came back to me. Let Rita Rollins come into any place, and five seconds later she's looking for the bedroom to powder and primp. You could make a bet on that little action, and never lose.

'Hold it, Rita,' I laughed. 'This is a business office. Besides, you look perfect. How are you any — '

It was then I saw that we were three, not two. He was a good-looking naval flier — a j.g. with enough fruit salad under his wings to tell he'd been around. His eyes at the moment, though, didn't go with the rest of his looks. They said how he'd love to shoot me down.

'Why, Harry, you silly!' Rita piped, pulling away from me. 'This is an old and dear friend. Harry, meet Gerry Barnes. Gerry, this is Harry Trent. He's on terminal leave with oodles of money. Isn't that thrilling? Let's have a party, shall we? I know just the — '

'Hold it, Rita,' I cut her off. 'Let us shake hands. Glad to meet you, Trent.'

At least it took the look out of his eyes. He grinned and we shook hands. 'Glad to meet you, too, Barnes,' he said. 'Rita's told me about you.'

'All lies,' I laughed, and hoped so. 'Rita's a great little kidder. But you probably know that by now.'

'Hey, my reputation!' Rita exclaimed. 'I only met Harry a couple of weeks ago. But isn't he a darling? We're having such fun.'

Sap I am, but I didn't like the way she looked at him — nor the way she hipped over to him and snuggled up. But Rita always did things to me. That was why I'd pulled away. 'Watch yourself, Trent,' I said with the big-brother chuckle. 'Going to be in town long?'

'Until I go broke or something,' he said, and looked down at Rita, not at me. 'Well, baby, I think your friend's swell. Shall we go?'

'But about a party!' Rita pouted and turned to me. 'Look, Gerry, how about Beth Price, and Clyde Mather, and Paula, and — '

I stopped her with both hands upraised. 'Slow down!' I said. 'Full stop. Maybe someday this week, but I'm a businessman today. Expecting an important call. Give Paula a ring one night, and we'll all do it like old times.'

Rita shrugged and went to work with purse, mirror and lipstick. 'Okay, okay,' she said, flat-voiced. 'I wouldn't keep you from Paula. How is she these days, anyway? High society as ever? I — '

'Hey, cut it!' I chided. 'You, of all people, the jealous type!'

'I always knew you never really got to know me,' she said, and gave me a look.

Then, turning to Trent, 'Come on, darling. You and I hate stuffy business-people, don't we?'

He looked at me over her shoulder. 'Be seeing you, Barnes,' he said.

'Sure, see you around . . . S'long, Rita.'

She made a face, crossed it off with a wink, and steered Trent out. I sat down and took a couple of deep breaths. Then I got up and opened the window to let the fresh air take the perfume and long-ago memories away. As I turned back to the desk, the phone rang. It was Paula at the other end. Her voice, or my phone, was a little off.

'Gerry? I've got that murder case for you. A man. He's — '

'W-what? Where? Who?'

'I don't know who he is,' she said. 'Only that he's here . . . and dead!'

'Where is here?' I barked. 'The Biltmore — '

'No, in my apartment!' she cut in. 'In my bedroom. Gerry, you must — '

And at that exact moment some dummy at the phone exchange yanked the wrong plug and broke the connection.

2

I spent a couple of minutes dialing and yelling into the dead phone before I gave up, grabbed my hat, and bolted for the office door. The door, however, opened in my face, and there stood the Empire State Building with a hat on. I actually went back a step, gaping — the guy was that big. Then his voice came all the way up from his shoes.

'You Barnes?'

'Yeah,' I said. 'But come back later. I'm in a hurry now.' I started to push by him, but he blocked the door opening with one arm and I had to back up.

'Then if you're Barnes, you're the guy I want,' he said. 'The boss wants to see you. Let's go. I got a car downstairs. Come on.' His hand came out four feet but I ducked it.

'Your boss can wait, too,' I grated, and rushed him.

Ever go head-on into a brick wall? Well,

I did. I sat down hard, and saw stars. When I could focus on his moon map, he was wagging his head.

'Look, I ain't got orders to hurt you, bud, so why get tough? The boss says just to bring you back. A right guy, the boss. He treats me good. So I don't disappoint him none, see?'

I was on my feet by the time he had finished. Still a little groggy, but getting smarter. I brushed some dust off my pants, then nodded. 'Okay, okay,' I said, backing toward my desk. 'Why didn't you say so? Be right with you. I want to get something first.'

I was in high gear before the last was out. I reached the desk in a back leap, yanked open the left side drawer, and grabbed out the gun I had a permit to carry.

'Now listen, stupid! I — '

And that was as far as I got. Nobody could move so fast, yet that ton of blubber did. I ducked and came up with the gun and my right foot together — a little commando trick I'd learned in the service. It didn't work. My foot caught him in the guts, but it was like kicking the side of a ship. And my gun didn't land. His big ham hands moved, and suddenly I didn't have the gun anymore. He had it.

'Are you nuts?' he asked me. 'These things can hurt guys. Now don't get me mad. The boss would get sore if I hadta blast you. Here. Just be a good Joe.'

Damned if the guy didn't bend over, pick up my hat, and hand it to me. I made to take it and swung with everything I had in my right. I almost broke my hand on his jaw. Then he smacked me and almost broke *my* jaw.

'Okay, you want me to beat you cold and lug you there? You comin', or you comin'?' He emphasized the last with a jab of my own gun into my ribs that hurt all the way through. I started to have sense then.

'You win,' I said. 'Who's your boss, and where does he live?'

'You'll be finding out both,' he said, and wrapped stovepipe fingers around my arm. 'Let's go.'

With that, he more or less jet-propelled me out of my own office and over to the elevator bank. All the time, he hung onto my arm. Had I made a break, he could have twisted it off just like that and slugged me over the head with it. Maybe the people in the elevator, or in the lobby, would have seen that he got his. But I like it much better with two arms.

So, though I burned with desire, I performed sensibly. Out in front was a big Caddy, with the twin brother of my baboon behind the wheel. He saw the hand around my arm and grinned.

'He don't wanna, Jake?' he said. And the voices matched too.

'Sure he wants to,' Jake replied, and pulled open the rear door. 'Get in, Barnes. Relax, too. Okay, Mike.'

Mike was way ahead of him. Before either Jake or I were seated, the car slid away from the curb, scared a taxi driver pink, and ripped down along the street. My hopes rose for a moment. The next cop would stop this fireman, and then would be my chance. But I was wrong. Mike must have been born with a steering wheel in his hand. He cut everything close but not so close as to raise a single eyebrow. So the only thing for me to do was to follow Jake's advice, and relax. Of course I could have whipped around on him and taken my gun away. It was in the side pocket next to me. But I just didn't feel like doing it at the moment.

'Tell me about your boss, Jake,' I tried to make conversation.

'He's a right guy,' Jake told me. 'You'll like him, bud. And he may do you some good. I got an idea, I have.'

'What kind of an idea?'

'Dough,' he practically whispered, as though the word was taboo. 'The boss is lousy with dough.'

'So am I,' I said quickly. 'And that gives me an idea, too. Have Mike drive me to another address first, and a hundred bucks is yours.'

Jake's face fell, and the corners of his mouth drooped.

'Two hundred bucks,' I upped it.

'Stop horsing. You ain't talking to another nut. Didn't I say the boss wants to see you, and he's a right guy?'

That record was getting scratchy, and there didn't seem to be anything I could do about it except shut up. So I did, and started paying some attention to where we were going. We were over on Riverside Drive and going north. At Ninety-sixth we turned and rolled over one block. And then we turned north again. We had traveled about two blocks when Jake pulled another of his cute little surprises. Before I knew what had happened, I was flat on my face on the floor, and Jake's number sixteen shoes were resting on my neck.

'Don't, bud,' he said as I started to struggle. 'This won't be for long. Just taking no chances, see?'

I didn't, but those number sixteens on my neck began to hurt like hell, so I quit. Then suddenly Jake removed them and hoisted me back up onto the seat. We were in an alley between two buildings and headed straight for a brick wall. I started to yell, but at that instant a part of said brick wall slid up, and we rolled to a smooth stop inside a basement garage.

'This way, bud,' Jake said.

He practically lifted me out and over to an elevator. We zoomed up for what seemed like a hundred floors, and stepped out into a half-moon-shaped room. It had no windows, but trick lighting made you think it did at first. The place was furnished with a couple of tables, half a dozen leather easy chairs, and an ornate desk over by the single door in the middle of the half round side. The lad sitting behind the desk looked at me with eyes like a rat.

'Here's the guy the boss wants to see, Kirby,' Jake said, and ushered me close. 'Tell him he's here, huh?'

Rat Eyes ignored Jake. He smiled at me. 'How do you do, Mr. Barnes. Just a minute, please.' He pressed one of several buttons and put his lips to a hush-o-phone. A moment or two later he nodded, and smiled at me again.

'Please have a chair, Mr. Barnes,' he said. 'Mr. White is taking his sun-lamp treatment right now, but he'll see you shortly.'

I jerked my arm free of Jake's grip and leaned over Kirby's desk. 'Look, you!' I clipped at him. 'This ape brought me here by force. You tell this White that he'll see me right now, and give me a damn good explanation, or I'll raise seventeen kinds of hell!'

'Mr. White is never disturbed during his sun-lamp treatments.' Kirby smiled. 'So you'd better start raising those seventeen kinds right now. Perhaps you'll help him, Jake?'

'Sure!' said Jake.

And before I could even turn, I was halfway across that foyer and slammed down into one of the leather chairs. Jake towered over me.

' 'Okay, bud,' he said, 'how do we start doing it, huh? You first, or me first?'

'You first!' I finally managed to wheeze out. 'You go to hell, and don't come back!'

'Nutty as a fruitcake!' Jake growled in disgust. 'Imagine! How the hell could I do that?'

I swore words at him nobody ever said before or since. Imagine, is right! Paula waiting with an unknown murdered man in her bedroom, and me waiting while the head of a gorilla farm took a sun-lamp treatment.

3

And wait I did. After about half an hour, a buzzer on Kirby's desk sounded, and a moment later he of the rat eyes looked over at Jake, lounging conveniently near me, and nodded.

'Mr. White will see Mr. Barnes now, Jake,' he said. 'Show him in.'

Jake was by my side and reaching for my arm. I ducked his reach and stood up.

'Save it, ape!' I growled. 'I can walk by myself.'

A couple of seconds later, we went through the heavy door, which opened when Kirby jabbed another one of his desk buttons. Beyond the door was a huge room fitted with floor-to-ceiling windows for two and three quarters of its sides. The blank side was the one through which we entered, and the other one quarter blank was taken up with a door that probably led to White's bedroom and such.

Through the windows you could see for miles and miles in any direction except west. But I wasted no time on the view. What caught my attention and held it was the man seated in a comfy chair over by the south windows. He was not good-looking, and he wasn't bad-looking, either. He was about my size, but five or ten years my senior. His complexion was what you'd expect in a guy who took sun-lamp treatments to save his winter-in-Florida tan.

There were two things, though, I noticed most. First, his eyes. They were like pink-tinted frosted glass, and just about as lifeless-looking. Secondly, his legs from his hips to his slipper toes were covered with a heavy robe. And although I couldn't tell for sure then, or during the talk we had, I had the feeling he was minus his right leg from the knee down.

He was having himself a highball when we came in. He put it down on a table by the arm of his chair and smiled at me. 'Come in, Mr. Barnes, do!' he said in a surprisingly pleasant voice. 'I'm so glad you came to see me. And my sincerest apologies, sir, for keeping you waiting so long.'

'*I'm* not glad, White,' I told him straight. 'This ape here dragged me in. Who do you think you are to — '

'My dear Mr. Barnes, I'm terribly sorry!' he exclaimed, and his voice was dripping. 'I merely sent Jake to give you my message. I have no phone here, you see. I dislike phones intensely. But I had no idea that . . . ' He paused and fixed his pink-frosted eyes on Jake, who was hovering around just in back of me. 'Jake, when will you ever learn?' he said sharply. 'I'm utterly ashamed of you! No wonder Mr. Barnes feels as he does. I don't blame him in the slightest. I — '

'But gee, Boss!' Jake growled in back of me. 'You said to bring him here, and I thought — '

'I do not pay you to *think!*' White cut him down. 'Only to do as I request. I'll speak to you later, Jake. Now go over there and sit down.'

'Sure, Boss, sure,' Jake mumbled.

Very pretty, but not smooth at all. When White returned, his apologetic eyes to mine, I shook my head. 'No go, White,' I said. 'Tell your mug to give me my gun. I'm leaving now.'

'Please, Mr. Barnes, I beg of you! I wouldn't have had this happen for the world. Good heavens, my dear sir, I wanted you to come here to *help* me. And to have you brought by force, against your will . . . '

Further words seemed too much for him. He sent a glare over at Jake that made even me feel funny. But it was still no go.

'You heard me, White. I'm leaving now. I wouldn't help you in anything on a bet. Next time, which there won't be, use your head!'

'*Mister* Barnes!' was all he said, but the way he said it was sort of like a hand closing around my throat. I can't explain it exactly, but it stopped me. And maybe Jake sliding like a big cat in front of the door helped to stop me, too. So I turned around. White was holding out a drink he had mixed. Pinch bottle and soda.

'Join me, Mr. Barnes,' he said with his smile. 'I insist that you do. And I must insist, also, that you at least listen to my story. It won't take long. Then you may leave . . . and do just as you please.'

An order and a threat. He didn't scare me, but I can be sensible on occasion, as well as a dope. Getting tough would achieve nothing. Jake was *too* tough. I walked over and accepted the drink — why turn down pre-war scotch? — and sat in a chair that flanked the other side of the table.

'Go ahead, talk,' I said. 'I'll listen, because I've *got* to. But that's all. Just keep that in mind from here in!'

'Thank you, and I shall, Mr. Barnes,' White smiled, leaning back. 'Let me start by saying that I have investigated you completely, sir. The help I desire — must have — demands a man of your natural qualities and acquired experience. I know there are a hundred private detectives in this city who can perform any number of baffling assignments, and perform them to a high degree of success. But you, Mr. Barnes, can perform, in this particular case, to the nth degree. If you get what I mean?'

He turned to look at me, and I let him look while I had another pull at my drink.

'Sorry, you said you'd only listen, didn't you?' he murmured, and returned his eyes to his drink. 'Very well, then, I'll get on with it. The problem is this. There's a man in this city I want you to find. At least, he was in this city three days ago. I feel quite sure, though, that he's still here. This man, sir, must be found at all costs. You must spare nothing in your efforts to find him. Your finding this man for me is the most vital thing of my entire life. And that, sir, is what I want you to do.'

He looked my way again, and then leaned over, took my glass and made me a refill. I didn't pick it up. Instead I stood up.

'Well, Mr. Barnes?' He smiled up at me.

I wanted to laugh at him. Was he nuts? Or did he think *I* was nuts? I pointed at my refill. 'You paid me for listening with the other one,' I said. 'Now I'm leaving.'

'Your fee, Mr. Barnes,' he said quietly,

and unsmiling, 'would be fifty thousand dollars.'

It was too sudden, and too unexpected. It jerked the rug from under my feet, and I sat down before I could check myself. I stared at White and watched the shadow of a smile play about the corners of his thin-lipped mouth. Now I was sure he was crazy. Fifty thousand dollars just to find a man?

'I told you that it was the most vital thing of my entire life, Mr. Barnes.'

I only half-heard him. I was off on a new train of thought. *Look at the picture,* I said to myself. *You, the most untried of all the private dicks, have been singled out. An ape bats your ears back and carts you here. You come up a back secret way into a screwy-looking layout. White is all soft-soap and tears about the way you've been treated, but you know he doesn't mean it any more than Hitler meant anything he ever said. Then you learn White just wants you to find a man. But . . . he'll pay fifty thousand dollars. Fifty thousand bucks! Why?*

I couldn't answer that, of course. And

then I began to get some ideas of my own. The answer and everything implied smelled of big doings. I looked at him and arched a brow. 'You want him pretty bad,' I said.

'I do,' he agreed. 'Are you interested?'

I shrugged, and without thinking reached for the refill he'd made. 'Maybe,' I said after a sip. 'Right now I'm thinking of the matter of a retainer.'

'How much?'

'Half. Twenty-five thousand. In cash.'

He nodded, and pulled a bunch of keys from his pocket. 'Jake!' he called, raising his voice.

'Yes, Boss?' the ape said, sliding over.

White tossed him the bunch of keys. 'Tell Kirby I want twenty-five thousand dollars,' he said. Then, turning to me, 'Any particular size of bills, Mr. Barnes? Large, small, or both?'

'Any old way,' I heard myself say.

He nodded at Jake, who went away. I had some more of my drink and let my eyes roam about the room. I didn't look at White. I didn't want him to see how neatly he had cleaned the bases. It was quite a room. Furnished to perfection in a man's style. Within arm's reach of every chair, or couch, in the place there was everything a man might need when relaxing. I caught myself wondering what his monthly liquor bill was; there were so many little rolling cabinets about. As a matter of fact, I wondered a whole lot of things about the room, White, and the whole set-up.

And then Jake came back in, a sheaf of bills in his hand. I could see that they were all crisp and new. White waved a hand at me. 'Give them to Mr. Barnes, please, Jake,' he said. Then to me, 'Count them, sir. And there's no need of a receipt, if one is supposed to be given in these matters.'

I took the bills and slipped them into my pocket without giving them a second look. 'I'll count them later,' I said easily. Then briskly, to let him know he hadn't bought anything yet, I said, 'Well, White, I've got a really important case awaiting my attention, so give me what facts you can, and as fast as you can. Who is he? What's he do? What's he look like? All the sorts of things that'll give me a lead or two.'

'My dear Mr. Barnes,' he laughed, 'you won't be able to earn your money that easily!'

'Meaning what?' I wanted to know. 'Naturally I don't expect to earn the money easily.'

'Naturally, Mr. Barnes. But it will be extremely difficult. For you see, sir . . . I haven't the faintest idea who he is!'

4

I felt the Scotch glass slipping through my fingers, so I squeezed them quick, and lifted it to my lips. When I put the glass down, it was empty. But even then, it hadn't given me much time to recover and do some fast thinking. Fifty thousand, twenty-five already paid in cash, to find somebody he didn't have the faintest idea who? I wondered if my first tab of White wasn't the right one.

'You don't know a thing about this man you want me to find?' I finally asked.

He shook his head. 'I didn't say that. I said I hadn't the faintest idea *who* he is. And that's true, I don't.'

'Then tell me what you do know, if anything,' I said.

He looked at his glass and made himself another. I squirmed at the delay. All the thoughts of Paula that had remained solid in the back of my brain came flooding forward. But I had to shove them back. There wasn't anything else I could do but wait until White gave Jake the nod.

'I know little,' White's voice finally came to me. 'He's young, or comparatively so, because he served in the war as a naval aviator. He's a New Yorker, or at least from this section of the country. That I judged from his voice when we talked. He — '

'Talked?' I cut in on him. 'I thought you said you didn't know him.'

'It was over the phone,' White said. Then, quickly, 'But not from here. Another spot. Anyway, as I was saying, he seemed to come from this part of the country. He served in the Pacific on a torpedo bomber, I believe he called it. And in February of 1944 he got shot down on some island in the Caroline group. Three months later he was rescued, and returned to active service. I must tell you that he gave me his name as Jordan, but I'm sure that's not his right name.'

'Why?' I got in when he paused for a drink. 'And how did you come to talk to him on the phone in the first place?'

'A week ago I received a letter containing an interesting proposition,' White said. 'It was signed, 'Jordan.' In it he stated that if I was interested in this proposition, to call him at a certain telephone number. I was interested and did make the call. It was to the Club Royale. The call was to be made at a certain time, by the way. A lady answered, and I asked for Jordan. A moment later, a man came on the phone. I suppose it was Jordan. I told him I was interested in his proposition, and to come see me first thing the next morning.'

White paused for a moment, and a change came into his eyes that gave war-veteran me the creeps. Melodramatic or not, it was a look of terrible death if I ever saw one.

'To prove I was seriously interested,' he suddenly went on as the creepy look vanished, 'I was to send him a certain sum of money. In cash. That night and to a downtown general delivery post office. To A. P. Jordan, to be exact. I did, and . . . and I also sent Jake down to follow

Jordan when he collected the money. Jake failed me. Jordan somehow collected it without Jake knowing it. An inexcusable blunder on my part to send Jake. But . . . well. Jake is so valuable to me in so many ways, I frankly didn't consider that he'd fail me. However, he did. And that's the end. I've called the Club Royale several times since. But whoever answered knew no Jordan, and never heard of any Jordan. And that, Mr. Barnes, is the limit of my knowledge of the affair.'

'What was the proposition?' I shot at him.

He turned his head slowly, and the frost in those eyes became solid, glittering ice. 'I'm paying you to find him, not to discuss with you my reasons why.'

'Okay, let it slide,' I said, and glanced at my watch. An hour and a half since Paula's call! I got quickly to my feet. 'How do I get in touch with you?'

He smiled and shook his head. 'You don't, Mr. Barnes. I'll keep in touch with you. Don't worry!'

Not much I wouldn't worry! I was

worrying already. 'Why did you select me, and why do you think I'll make good?'

'Your *ego*, sir. And for various other reasons . . . One, because you have all the money you desire, therefore your motivating force is purely a personal one. Another, having served in Intelligence . . .'

'Wrong,' I cut in. 'It was the Office of Strategic Services.'

He waved that aside. 'Same thing, practically. Anyway, I know all about your war service, and that you have connections in Washington that no other private detective has. I think you can trace this Jordan — find his real name, and so forth — through Washington with the data I've given you on his crash and rescue. Good luck, Barnes. And I do want results.'

It was thinly veiled, that last crack, but I ignored it. 'And when I do find him . . . ?' I said, straightening my coat.

'I'll know when you do, Mr. Barnes, and you'll be given your instructions then. Jake! Take Mr. Barnes to wherever he wishes to go.'

I wasn't in the mood to argue. All I

wanted was out, and fast. So I turned and walked with Jake out into the half-moon-shaped room and over to the elevator. As the door closed behind me, I could have sworn I heard a phone bell ring back where White was.

We went down the way we had come up. Mike was there behind the Caddy's wheel, but he'd turned the car around somehow. Jake opened the rear door and motioned me in.

'In and flat, bud,' he said with a smile. 'But only for a couple of minutes.'

I could have argued that, but what was the point? My head hurt enough as it was. So I got in, and got down on my face.

And Mike started us rolling. A few minutes, later when Jake hoisted me back up onto the seat, the car was over on Riverside Drive.

'Where to, bud?' he grunted at me.

'Ninety-sixth and Park,' I told him, holding out my hand. 'And my gun!'

He shook his big head and snorted.

'Still nutty, huh? Ninety-sixth and Park, Mike!'

I sighed and settled back on the

cushions and gave myself up to dozens and dozens of head-aching thoughts, all of which were just plain, screwy, cock-eyed, and unbelievable. However, there was one thing that was believable. That was the bulge that twenty-five thousand dollars made in my jacket pocket. And yet again when I pressed my arm against it, it seemed the most unbelievable item of all.

'You goin' to find this guy, bud?'

Jake's question pulled me out of my thoughts. 'A cinch,' I ribbed him.

'The guy must be a ghost,' he said. 'And you know something else? The boss just threw away that dough, giving it to you, bud.'

'So?' I grunted.

'You're nutty, but you may be a good dick. But that ain't what I mean. That guy blew with the dough, sure. I bet he's in California now. The boss is a sucker for new ideas, see? Why, he'll go for — '

'Clam, Jake! Ya hear me — clam!'

That was from Mike up front. Jake's face went dark, and his eyes bugged. 'Aw, I wasn't saying anything,' Jake growled as he relaxed.

'That's what I mean!' Mike cracked without turning his head. 'You never do. So shut up!' Before Jake could say anything more, Mike swung the car over to the curb and stopped. 'Ninety-sixth and Park,' he said.

It was, and as I opened the door and got out without feeling Jake's hairy fingers gripping my arm, it was like walking out of prison. Then I turned and stuck my head and hand back in. 'The gun,' I said.

He pulled it from his pocket and started to toss it to me but changed his mind. Instead he broke it, dumped the shells out into his hand, snapped it shut and handed it to me, muzzle first.

'Just on account of you're extra nutty, bud,' he said. Then, with a grin, 'But no hard feelings, huh?'

I slipped the gun into my pocket and stood there looking at him. 'I don't like dumb apes shoving me around!' I said, and I made my voice plenty hard. 'The next time, you big ape, I'm going to cut you down to my size and beat the living hell out of what's left. And I hope the

36

next time is soon!'

'No kiddin'?' he echoed. 'Look, the boss gives me Thursday nights off. I always play some pool and have a few beers at Marty's over on Eighth. Maybe you could drop around next Thursday, huh?'

I didn't have the opportunity to accept the invitation. Brilliant Gerry Barnes was being a chump twice in one day. The flat of Jake's hand shot out, smacked my kisser dead center, and I went flying flat on my back on the sidewalk. The Caddy slid away, and as I struggled to my feet, Jake leaned out of the car window and waved a handkerchief.

'I'll be seeing a lot of you, Daisy!' he hooted.

5

I dusted myself down and walked to the next block. Here I hailed a cab and rode it to Paula's apartment building on the east Eighties. It was one of those cooperative affairs with a private elevator for a few of those who paid top rent. Paula was one of those few. When I'd paid off the cab, I took a quick look around, and a deep breath of relief. There were several cars parked along the curb, but none of them belonged to the New York Police Department. So I ducked in the side door and took one of the private elevators to Paula's apartment on the twenty-fourth floor, northeast corner.

She answered my ring in two seconds flat. Apart from a slight tinge of worry in her lovely eyes, she was her usual beautiful self. Her voice wasn't the same as she stepped back to let me in and quickly closed and chain-bolted the door.

'So nice of you to come so soon, Mr.

Barnes!' she said, and let the icicles fall where they would. Then, breaking a little, 'Where the devil have you been, Gerry?'

I took her in my arms and held her hard.

'Easy,' I soothed. 'I got held up, but I'm here now. Just relax. Everything's going to be okay.'

She pushed out of my arms in an angry movement. 'Sure, sure, everything's swell! Twice a week I find a dead man in my bedroom. My God, Gerry, I've been going — '

She stopped short and looked closely at my left temple, where sweet little Jake had left a lump. 'Hey! You've been in a fight! What happened?'

Her sudden concern for me over her own troubles made me kiss her again. 'Tell you later,' I said, and walked her out of the foyer. 'In the bedroom, huh? You stay here, Paula. Mix us a drink. We both need one. But I'll take a look first.'

I gave her a gentle push toward the cabinet of drink makings, and turned right toward the bedroom door. It was only partly closed, so I pushed it open with my foot. The bed was to the left as you entered. A huge one, because Paula liked that kind. The room was full of trick boudoir furniture that Paula had designed herself. A sight to see, was Paula's bedroom, but I didn't waste time ogling.

The corpse was on the bed, sprawled flat on his back across it, with the lower half of his legs dangling over the edge. He had brown hair, and brown eyes that were open and glassy now. He looked about twenty-seven, and even in death his ordinary-looking face bore the telltale marks of one who hit the wild spots and the bottle far beyond the danger point. His suit was a gray herringbone, new, but rumpled now; as though his killer had given him a thorough frisk after the deed had been done.

The handle of the knife was sticking up out of the base of his throat. Collar, shirt, and part of his camel-hair vest were stiff with dried blood. There were also some splashes of dried blood on the bedspread.

I was jolted when I looked closely at the knife handle. It was a native-made bone-handled pearling knife I had sent to Paula from the Fiji Islands.

For several minutes I just stood there staring down at the stiff. He was a total stranger to me. Was he really a total stranger to Paula, too? As the question passed through my mind, I cursed myself for the heel I could be, even in my thoughts. Then I went through the stiff's pockets. And I could have saved myself the trouble. An ordinary pocket knife, a dollar and seven cents in change, an unused unmarked handkerchief, a silver lighter, a half-filled pack of Luckies, and an average-priced wristwatch were all the knickknacks he had on him. The suit label was Howard Clothes.

Having handled the stuff, I left it in a little pile on the bed beside him. I slowly looked about the room, but all I saw was that Paula's lower bureau drawer was halfway open. I took one more look at the corpse, bit my lip because of the nagging worry that was ticking over in the back of my head, and went out into the living room. Paula was on the couch over by a brace of French windows that looked out over a million rooftops to the East River, and Long Island beyond. On the coffee table in front of her were two drinks, and the fixings to make more if wanted.

I sat down beside her, grinned, kissed her, and had some of my drink. Both her lips and the drink were cold.

'Have some,' I said, pointing at hers. 'And then tell me about it.'

'There's hardly anything to tell. I came home here, found him, damn near fainted, and called you.'

'I thought you were going to the Biltmore,' I said.

'In these rags?'

'These rags' looked perfect on her to me. But a woman is a woman, so I let it pass.

'Door locked when you came here?' I asked.

'Yes,' she said into her glass.

I frowned, trying to figure a way to express my thoughts so that Paula wouldn't blow up, or crown me, or both. 'When did you leave here this morning?' I started across the thin ice.

'Around nine. Why?'

'And came back when?' I took another step.

I heard her softly suck air through her nose. An old familiar danger signal. I held my eyes on the desk and waited.

'Twenty minutes after I left you,' came the tight reply. 'At half past two, to be exact. And I can prove where I was *every minute* in between, too. Damn you, Gerry Barnes . . . '

I turned quickly and grabbed her hands as lightning sparks shot out of her eyes. 'Paula, cut it!' I snapped, and squeezed. 'I know goddam well you didn't do it, darling. But there are questions I've got to ask, if I'm going to be able to do anything about this. Dammit, Paula . . . '

She jerked her hands free of mine and went over to her purse on a near table. She fumbled in it for a moment, then came back and threw a penny in my lap.

'You're hired, Detective Barnes!' she clipped out. 'There's your retainer. The other four cents when you've cleared me of this terrible thing. All right! Ask your questions.'

'All right, Miss Grant,' I said. 'Have

you ever seen him before?'

She took all of twenty seconds before she said, 'No, I don't *think* so.'

'Don't *think* so?' I echoed, flaring. 'You said on the phone that — '

'I did not!' she cut in viciously. 'I said I didn't know *who* he was. That's different!'

Private Detective Barnes went back to second base in sullen silence. And then both of us damn near dropped our drinks as the silence was shattered by the doorbell. We stared at each other, and I'll never see Paula closer to fainting than I did at that moment.

'My God, what'll we do?' she whispered.

I said the first thing that popped into my mind. 'Let it ring.'

It did, again, and Paula started trembling. 'Better answer it, Gerry,' she said. 'It may be someone from downstairs. And they know that I'm here. Oh, dammit! Answer it, anyway.'

Quickly, I ran over and closed the bedroom door. Then I went through the foyer, took off the chain-bolt, and opened up.

'Ah hah, and uh-huh! And what we can guess about you, taking so long!'

It was Rita Rollins, quite a few seas over. And with her were Trent, Beth Price, and Clyde Mather. The last two I could thumbnail-sketch in a jiffy. Betty Price was one of the current about-the-town cocktail gals. Her old man owned a string of race horses and lots of money for his daughter to sling around on clothes, cars, and all the rest of it. Actually, she was a fairly nice kid. Just a couple of screws loose, that's all. Or maybe she could act and make you think so. I never tried to figure it out. I wasn't ever interested enough to put her phone number down in my little black book.

Clyde Mather was different. He topped any one of our wartime running-around gang by at least ten years. He was on the plump side, but he managed to hold it in check. He had money, and didn't seem to work. He also had a trick little mustache I had often wanted to knock off. But maybe that was because he was always trying to play brother, and you know what, to Paula.

Well, I wanted to slam the door in the faces of the whole lot of them, but little chance I got. They swept by me in nothing flat, and all of them, save Trent, gurgled inane greetings at Paula in the same breath. I shut the door quickly and sprinted in after them.

'Darling, darling!' Rita was gushing at Paula. 'It's so marvelous to see you again! And I bet I look a sight!'

She stopped and half-turned, and my heart banged up into my throat. The bedroom, and the old ritual! I moved quickly to head her off. But she just smiled at Trent right behind her and put out her hand. While she introduced Trent to Paula, my heart worked its way back down again. And started burning, because of the way Trent looked at Paula and smiled. Rita saw it, too, and practically yanked him away.

'Come on, Paula, and you, darling,' she burst out with a flash of eyes my way. 'Harry here wants to sit in on one of our old win-the-damn-war parties. We — '

'Look, Rita,' I said, but that's as far as I

got. She went running right over my words.

' — have reserved one of those cute little rooms at Teddy Dane's Inn. We'll split up the cars, and all go together now. Come on, one and all. This little gal is really celebrating tonight!'

'Celebrating what, Rita?' Paula managed to get in.

'Oh, you haven't heard, have you, darling?' Rita said. 'Well, my tryout at the Club Royale was a success. Yes, sir! I'm going to get a signed, sealed and delivered contract to sing regular with Bert Mann's band. Yeah man, and Mann! Give the little gal a great big hand, and let's go. Tonight I sing for free for yooze guys!'

Paula smiled, and spoke due congratulations. But at the same time she flashed a look my way. I caught the plea and took charge. I went over to Rita and hugged her.

'That's for me!' I exclaimed to one and all. Then, quickly looking at my watch with a frown, 'But you all shove along and we'll meet you at Dane's. It's five now. Meet you there at six-thirty. Right?'

'Oh, come with us now, Gerry!' Betty Price pleaded and pouted at the same time.

'Nope, Beth,' I said. 'A businessman, I. Nine to six. But Paula and I will be there.'

'Nice work, if you can get it!'

That from Trent with a look on his face. Maybe I would have snapped a crack, and looked stupid, if Clyde Mather hadn't been bending and drooling all over Paula just then.

'But *you* can come now, my dear, can't you?' he was simpering. 'In my new car? I was around this morning to show it to you, but you were out. Please?'

'No, Clyde, dear, I can't,' Paula said. 'I have some things to do first. *Musts*, you know.'

Dear Clyde argued some more, and so did all of the others. But eventually, with a stack of cross-my-heart promises, I was able to shoo them to the door, and outside. Once they were gone, I leaned for a moment against the door and removed more than a few drops of sweat from my heated brow. When I went back into the living room, Paula was recovering with the aid of another drink. I debated a moment whether to have one myself. But I decided that it was time to do the sensible thing before the Seventh Regiment barged in on us. I went over to the phone and picked it up.

'Gerry!' Paula got out in a startled voice. 'What are you going to do?'

I first dialed the number, and then smiled over at her.

'What all *smart* people do when there's been a murder,' I said. 'Call the police.'

6

When the apartment doorbell rang, I swallowed the heel of my drink, gave Paula a reassuring pat on the cheek, and answered it.

There were four men in the hall, all of whom I knew — well or otherwise. One was Lieutenant Frank Bierman of Homicide, an average-looking man crowding fifty. Another was Doctor Sperry, the department's medical examiner. And another was Sergeant Goff, who could find a fingerprint in the haystack before you could find the needle with a magnet.

The fourth chap I was both pleased and displeased to see. He was Bill Hatch of the *Globe*. I was pleased to see him because Bill's a swell guy, and a pal of long standing. I was displeased to see him because he was there as a part of his job. I had hoped to hold the affair from the papers until I had at least got things somewhat squared away. But that was that, so I opened the door wider and stood to the side.

'Come in, Lieutenant, gentlemen,' I said.

The first three nodded, murmured something and entered. Bill Hatch paused beside me and gave me the lifted brow.

'Sherlock's first case, eh?' he grunted. 'Luck, kid.'

I said, 'Thanks,' and shut the door and hurried past the parade into the living room. Paula had risen to her feet, beautiful and calm.

'Paula,' I said, 'Lieutenant Bierman, Doctor Sperry, Sergeant Goff, and Bill Hatch. Gentlemen, Miss Paula Grant.'

I gave the boys a few seconds to be polite, and then took a couple of steps toward the bedroom. 'This way, Lieutenant,' I said. 'The body's — '

'One minute, Barnes!'

I thought I was handling it smoothly, so the sharp voice turned me around in surprise. Bierman crooked a finger for me to come back.

'Being dead a little longer won't make

any different to him,' Bierman said. Then, smiling at Paula, 'You found the dead man, I gather. Tell me just how, please?'

Paula seated herself and gave him her best smile. 'I left the apartment at about nine this morning, Lieutenant,' she said. 'I returned at half past two, and found him there in my bedroom.'

Bierman looked at his wristwatch and nodded.

'I see,' he said. 'And when you found him?'

'As soon as I recovered from the slightly unusual experience, I called Mr. Barnes at his office,' Paula said. Then, letting fly the barb, 'Mr. Barnes has opened a private investigator's office, you know.'

'Yes, I know,' Bierman murmured with as much interest as if I'd got my shoes shined. 'You called, let us say about quarter of three, Miss Grant. And Barnes arrived here when?'

Paula smiled bittersweetly. 'Oh, not for a long, long time afterward, Lieutenant!' she said, wide-eyed. 'Almost half past four, I think it was.'

'And while you waited?' Bierman pushed on.

Paula fluttered her hands. The eternal helpless female act, damn her lovely hide!

'Why, I just waited, Lieutenant,' she said. 'I was truly petrified. I didn't dare move from where I am now. You see, I was counting on Mr. Barnes coming quickly and giving me the advice I needed.'

I could have given her some swell advice right there and then, but I didn't. Besides, Bierman had turned to me. His eyes fastened on Jake's goose-egg gift, and then moved to mine.

'Ran into a door, you were in such a hurry, Barnes?' he asked pleasantly.

'No, a client,' I told him. 'An insistent one. Took longer than I expected to shake him off.'

Maybe it was the start and finish of a grin I saw on his face. I couldn't tell. He looked at his watch again.

'Your advice to Miss Grant took three quarters of an hour?'

I looked at my own watch and

shrugged. 'I guess it did. Plus the time you took getting here.'

Bierman nodded and let his eyes wander about the room. When they came back to the coffee table with Paula's and my empty glasses, he frowned. Then he made a face as though he'd sucked a lemon.

'I hate the scientific who-done-it method,' he grunted as though to himself. 'But it does crop up now and then. Six different brands. Three with lipstick. We're not your first visitors?'

I followed his pointing finger to the big glass ash tray on the coffee table. Paula, me, Rita Rollins, and the others had all used it. Secret One I was going to keep went up in smoke.

Frank Bierman, of Homicide, was nobody's dope. Neither am I, I hope. So I told him about Rita and the others barging in. He didn't act as though that was important. And somehow I was sort of relieved.

'All right, Doctor, Goff,' he said, and started toward the bedroom.

I took a few quick steps to catch up

with him, but he stopped me with a gesture.

'Thanks, but we can find the way, Barnes,' he said. 'And by the by, you've made a good start in your new profession.'

I looked at him, not catching it.

'Calling as soon as you did,' he said with the briefest of smiles. 'It's always best to give the police an even start. You might bear that in mind.'

Advice or a hint? I didn't know. I felt silly and sore I couldn't join them. I just nodded and went back to Bill Hatch and Paula. When I heard the bedroom door close, I gave her the snarl. 'Thanks!' I grated. 'That made me look just fine!'

'Well, why did you take so damn long?' she blazed at me. 'You haven't told me yet!'

'Children, children!' Bill Hatch broke in. 'As an interested party . . . may I have a drink?'

Paula just waved a hand at the mixings and kept her blazing eyes on me. 'Well?' she demanded. 'Just what did happen? Was the client a blonde?'

'That,' I growled, 'is none of your damn business, now!'

She flashed the battle signals, snatched the drink Bill had made for himself, and took a pull. Then she gave it back to him.

'Perhaps not, Investigator Barnes!' she snapped some more. 'But I bet a certain *real* detective I could name will make it *his* business! And — '

'Could you sell an ardent admirer a fifth of this stuff, Paula darling?' Hatch broke in, sloshing his drink around. 'But first, tell me, what's the guy's name?'

'We don't know,' I said without looking at him. 'Now listen, Paula — '

'No name?' Hatch stopped me. 'But all people have names, even dead ones. It's a law of the land.'

I cooled down fast and turned to him. 'Look, Bill, the whole thing is nuts. Every word Paula told Bierman is true. I mean . . . save for her dirty cracks at me. But honest — she doesn't know the guy, and neither do I. And look, you've got to soft-pedal it in your paper. Paula's — '

'The woman of my dreams,' the crazy coot got in, leering at her. 'And maybe for a fifth of this — '

'Stop clowning!' I barked. 'This crazy mess is damn serious. Now, Bill — '

He stopped me with an upraised hand and put down his empty glass with the other. 'So am I serious, fire-eater,' he said, and he wasn't joking. 'Paula's the woman of my dreams, and though you're a nightmare at times, I still like you plenty. That's why I made Bierman bring me along when your call came in. To find out what the hell, and do what I could for Paula. As for you — a tip, pal.'

'Meaning?' I said, and waited.

'May I, dearest?' he said to Paula, and mixed one before she could nod. Then, squinting over his drink, to me: 'My friend, Frank Bierman's forgotten more about the detecting business than you'll ever learn. Remember that. Remember, also, that all police detectives resent private detectives. And quite naturally so. In a word, Gerry, stop licking Bierman's boots!'

'Why, you — you — ' I exploded, and couldn't finish.

'Nuts!' Hatch said flatly. 'To me you

were trying to be the nice, polite guy that you are. To Bierman, you were fawning. Believe me!'

'Hear, hear!' Paula chirped up. 'Stick to your glen, fawn!'

I was a quarter of the way to making it three murders when the bedroom door opened and Bierman came out alone. I was so stuck on the merry-go-round that I whirled to him and blurted out my little piece. 'Fifteen minutes either way of ten o'clock, wasn't it?' I fairly shouted at him.

His brows went up in mild surprise. And with a slight bit of admiration, too, I thought. His words proved my thought correct.

'How did you know, Barnes?'

I had a firmer grip on myself by then, and played it through as I should have. 'For the last four years, I've seen death in all its stages. I learned to tell a few things about a corpse. What did Doc Sperry say?'

Bierman walked over, cast a longing look at the drink in Hatch's hand, and lighted a cigarette. 'Around ten,' he said. Then, to stop any crowing, 'But he isn't sure. Excuse me, please. Keep right on talking. But not so loud.'

We watched him walk over to the phone. The two phones, I should say. He used the apartment house-phone first. And though my ears stuck out a mile, I pretended not to listen. I could have saved myself the act. I didn't hear a word of the two dial-phone calls he made, either. Then he rejoined us, frowning and thoughtful. But he had a smile for Paula.

'Was your door locked when you returned?' he asked.

She nodded, and told him what she had told me.

'Anyone else who would possess a key?' he asked lightly.

But Paula didn't take that lightly. She showed Bierman a bit of the eye lightning, and I felt like grinning. 'A long-standing custom in the Grant family, Lieutenant,' she said sweetly. 'We *never* lend out house keys. Particularly to men.'

Bierman grinned at that one, and I took the moment's pause to stick in my oar. 'There's such a thing as skeleton keys,' I said.

I thought I heard Bill Hatch groan. Anyway, Bierman's grin went away. 'That is so, isn't it?' he grunted. 'Tell me,' he went on to Paula, 'I understand the dead man is a total stranger. To both of you, in fact. But have you ever seen him before? When he was alive?'

Paula was hesitant and thoughtful. I could almost hear Bierman's brains click.

'I really don't know,' Paula answered eventually. 'I'm just not sure. Perhaps I did meet him when he was alive. But where, or when, or how, or what it was all about, I haven't the faintest.'

'Well, we'll find out who he is — was,' Bierman said quietly. 'Then perhaps you'll be able to recall something.'

'I certainly will if I can!' Paula said. And I could see that Bierman knew she meant it.

And I could see something else. Paula was really beginning to feel the strain, and was battling the jim-jams inside. I could tell by the tightening of the corners of her eyes. I opened my mouth to speak, but Bierman beat me. Still to Paula.

'The murder weapon,' he said. 'Have — '

'Mine,' she stopped him, and nodded at me. 'Gerry, I mean Mr. Barnes, sent it to me from the Fiji Islands three years ago. And I used it for a letter opener . . . on my desk over there.' Paula pointed at the ornate but cute-looking desk in the corner. Her finger shook a little, so I put in my word.

'That's right, Bierman,' I said, purposely dropping his title for Hatch's benefit. 'And I guess that's the whole story. Someone unknown brought somebody else unknown in here, and killed him. Now, look . . . '

'Just a minute,' he stopped me pleasantly. 'About this client who . . . delayed you. Who was he?'

Bill Hatch's word still rankled, so I played the clam. 'It's not necessary to reveal his name,' I said. 'I didn't take his case. And besides, he could have no possible connection with this business.'

'Why not?' Bierman had a tone of voice that could really grind you.

'It was a hotel-room-keyhole case against his wife,' I said, and made a vague gesture. 'Does that connect up with this?'

Bierman looked at the lump on my head and pursed his lips. 'Probably not,' he said after a pause. Then, bringing his eyes to mine, 'You were going to say something else?'

'Yes,' I said, and nodded at Paula. 'Miss Grant. She's had a pretty trying experience, and I imagine she doesn't want to hang around here any longer than she has to. As we've told you all we can, do you mind my taking Miss Grant out of here? For a little while anyway.'

Bierman looked at her and his face softened a little. 'Take her to where?' he asked, swinging back to me.

'The Biltmore cocktail lounge,' Paula beat me, and stood up. 'Nick or Angelo can mix me just what I need badly now. And you don't mind, do you, Lieutenant? Just a little air . . . and something by Nick or Angelo? Cross my heart, I've told you everything.'

He frowned, and I thought he was going to veto it. But Lieutenant Frank Bierman was a man of many surprises.

'Why not?' he said. Then, almost wistfully, 'Wish I could go with you.

Matter of fact, I don't need any of you for a while.'

The last was with Bierman's eyes fixed on Bill Hatch. The *Globe*'s man grinned and wagged a finger.

'What *you* think, but skip it,' he said. And with a nod toward the bedroom, 'I'll just take a peek at the dear departed, and then go where you want me to go, with them.'

Bierman grunted, and made a motion for him to step on it. I looked over at Paula for the thanks smile. But my beautiful two-timer was giving it to the New York Detective Bureau instead.

7

Nick was on duty and he spotted us right away. He came over fast, his dark eyes and white teeth showing his honest-to-goodness pleasure.

'Miss Grant, so nice to see you. And you, Mr. Barnes. And Mr. Hatch! Come with me. I have just the table.'

It was. In a corner of the lounge. Leather chairs with arms, not the straight backs. And plenty of room to stretch and rubber around. Before we had settled down and taken a breath, Nick had zipped off and zipped back with popcorn, potato chips, salted nuts, and cocktail napkins. The looks we got from other tables made me expect autograph books almost any second.

Nick, the perfect, chatted a brief moment and then looked from Paula to me. 'The usual?' he asked.

'This tall, Nick,' Paula smiled at him, and showed him with her hands.

I nodded, and Nick looked at Bill Hatch. 'And you, Mr. Hatch?'

'The usual, by all means, whatever it is,' Bill said. 'But bigger. Mr. Barnes is paying for it.'

Nick joined in the lame laugh and went away. I took some salted nuts and popped them into my mouth but forgot to close it for an instant. On the far side of the lounge, and beyond the partition of potted plants, I suddenly saw the face of a man walking by just for an instant, and then he was lost to view. But in that instant, I thought I was getting a look at a certain Mr. White in profile.

'What is it, Gerry?'

Paula's voice brought me out of it and closed my mouth on the salted peanuts. 'Nothing,' I said. 'Thought I saw somebody I knew. I was wrong.'

'But startled for a moment,' murmured Hatch on my right. 'It wasn't the client of the goose egg on your temple, was it?'

'No,' I told him, and reached for more nuts.

'We're a patient pair; Paula and I,' Hatch said. 'When do we hear about that client story, anyway?'

'Yes, when?' Paula said, taking a sarcastic interest. 'You swear she wasn't a blonde? They do hit hard.'

Paula's wisecracks, plus the fact that nobody likes to talk about the shoving around he got, decided me that what had happened between Paula's phone call and my arrival at her apartment was nobody's damn business except mine. At least for the time being. But I yearned to take the twenty-five thousand from my pocket and slap it down in front of their popping eyes. Instead I ignored Paula and turned to Hatch.

'Frankly, I was a little surprised Bierman let us go,' I said. 'Do you suppose he really believes we told him all? Which, incidentally, we did.'

Before Bill could answer, Nick arrived with the drinks. They were tall, and one hundred percent inviting.

'I stopped trying to figure Bierman's moves on a case long ago,' Hatch said when Nick had left. 'As you will, too, before this case is cleaned up. My guess, though, is that he could see Paula needed a change of scenery. And you taking her out for the change would also take you out from under his feet.'

'Thanks!' I growled. 'And I think you're smart at your job, too. Drinking instead of phoning in to your paper.'

He saluted me with lifted glass and grinned. '*Touché*, almost, pal,' he said. 'The *Globe* is a morning sheet. Remember? Plenty of time. However, to be in at the start of an unknown murder isn't important. The real story is the solving of it.'

'Then you should have stayed with the lieutenant, Bill,' Paula commented.

'No, sweetheart,' Hatch said. 'This gentleman here, with his heart now showing in his eyes, will crack this case.'

'Hey!' I half-laughed, half-growled. 'It was understood I'd pick up the check.'

'Nothing to do with it,' Bill said, and still looked at Paula. 'Beautiful, write the man a check as a retainer. His first case. Believe me, it will be money well spent.'

'What?' Paula cried, and stopped her glass halfway to her luscious lips. 'You mean, to prove I didn't do it?'

'Nuts to that!' Hatch snapped. 'To make it official. Not for love, but a real business assignment. And his first of many, we pray. So . . . '

'I'm already retained by the lady,' I cut in, and fished Paula's penny from my pocket and bounced it in the palm of my hand. 'Four more, mind you, when I've cracked it.'

'*If* blonde clients give you the time,' Paula said, and glared.

'Oh, for God's sake!' I snapped, and then stopped short as Hatch's shoe toe hit my shin.

'I'm serious, Paula,' he said. 'And I never like to be this way. But I was in the Pacific, too. With Gerry some of the time. This is the kind of problem he's cut out for. To a 'T.' I mean it. God knows how he'll crack it, but . . . Well, I just feel that he will. So, both of you, stop giving each other the back of your hand. And where the hell is Nick?'

'Right here, Mr. Hatch,' came that pleasant, soft voice out of nowhere. And sure enough, there Nick was.

'Another for me, Nick,' Bill said. Then,

glancing at ours not a quarter gone, 'And a straw each for the lady and gent. It appears to sting their chapped lips.'

Very unfunny, but it seemed to ease the high-voltage tension that enveloped our little threesome table. I laughed and reached my hand across the table to Paula.

'The guy's talking through his hat,' I said. 'Just like in his lousy column. But I guess we *have* been acting like kids. Shake, darling?'

'*You* have, anyway,' she said. But she took my hand, and the pressure of her fingers told me almost as much as her eyes.

'Love, it's wonderful!' Hatch murmured. Then his face became serious. 'Okay, Gerry,' he said to me. 'Any ideas, and if so, just what?'

'No ideas at all,' I lied in a sad voice. 'This one is going to be tough. Your look at him give you any ideas?'

'None,' Bill said absently. 'And I doubt that Bierman got any either. As you say, this one is going to be tough.'

Conversation was dropped for a

moment while Nick served Bill his second. He took a sip and looked at me queerly, then suddenly switched his gaze to Paula's face.

'Yeah, a screwy set-up,' he said. 'You two don't happen to be giving an old friend of the family the runaround?'

'Don't be silly, Bill!' Paula scoffed. 'Believe me, you know every bit as much about the crazy thing as I do.'

'Ditto,' I said into my drink. 'Or pretty close to it, anyway.'

Hatch's brows went up quickly.

'Yes? Give, my friend.'

I shook my head and grinned. Then I cut short the grin when I saw the tired look on Paula's face. I was about to ask her if she wanted another, when she spoke to Hatch.

'How good is your drag with Lieutenant Bierman, Bill? Would he do you a favor?'

'Depends on the favor. What is it?'

'I somehow don't relish the idea of sleeping in my own bed tonight,' Paula said, and tried to smile. 'Do you think the lieutenant would mind if I took a room

70

here? I can send one of the hotel people up for my overnight bag. I always keep it packed. What do you think?'

Hatch drained his glass in one long gulp and stood up. 'For you, fair one, I can give it a try,' he said. 'I'll call him. He's probably still there.'

'You're a dear,' Paula said, and crinkled her eyes. 'If only you didn't have a wife and six kids!'

'Seven kids, madam,' Bill said. 'Stick here.'

When Hatch had gone, I looked at Paula and smiled kind of crookedly. 'I should have thought of that,' I said. 'I'm sorry, dear.'

'I'm sorry too, darling,' she said, and squeezed my hand. Then, 'You lied to Bill, didn't you? You do have an idea?'

'Call it a hunch,' I said. 'Don't ask, though, because I can't even put it into words that make sense to myself. I've got to work on it for a spell.'

Paula smiled and nodded understandingly. And then she promptly went right back to being a woman again. 'Gerry,' she said, and didn't look at me, 'about that client who held you up so long. Was it really a . . . '

I didn't hear the rest, because at that exact instant my eyes met those of Mr. White. He was standing way over where the waiters go for the drinks, but behind the potted plants. One flash of his face and then he was gone again. I didn't even waste time making excuses to Paula. I got up quickly and went out the lounge exit on our side. Walking fast, I followed the border of potted plants all the way around to the other side. And saw nobody who looked like White. I squinted through the opening of a couple of potted plants and took a good look at everybody in the lounge. No Mr. White.

Then Nick's voice spoke behind me. 'Something the matter, Mr. Barnes? You and Miss Grant want another?'

Nick had come out of the waiters' entrance. The only way White, if it had been White, could have avoided meeting me was to have ducked in there.

'Nick,' I said, and pointed, 'pop back in there, will you? I'm looking for somebody, and I think he ducked in there. About my size, but a bit older. Brown hair with a couple of streaks of white. On the distinguished side. Take a look, will you, like a pal?'

'Sure, sure, Mr. Barnes!' And Nick was gone. He was back in a couple of minutes, shaking his head. 'Nobody like that in there, Mr. Barnes,' he said. 'I asked a couple of the waiters, too. Of course, though . . . '

'Of course what, Nick?'

He pointed to a closed door to the left inside the entrance. 'He could have gone through there. That leads to the kitchens and the locker rooms. You want me — '

'No, let it ride,' I stopped him. 'Thanks, Nick. And sure, get one more for Miss Grant and myself. And you'd better make it another one for Hatch, too.'

Nick said he would right away, and I went back to Paula. Bill had made his call and was with her. Both of them cocked eyebrows at me.

'Sorry I tore off, Paula,' I said. 'Thought I saw an old Guadalcanal pal. Jeff Heath. But I was wrong. You ever meet up with Jeff Heath, Bill?'

'No, I never did,' he said, and gave me a look that told me to do better than that next time. 'But Bierman says it's okay for Paula to park here.'

'Swell! Did he say anything else? Wants to see me, or something?'

'Your name wasn't mentioned,' Hatch said, and gave me a teasing grin. 'But he knows where you live when he wants you. Ah! I am saved the embarrassment of asking!'

The last was because of Nick's arrival. Hatch took his and in two tries it was gone. 'Well, the poor people will now go to work,' he said. 'Besides, to coin a phrase, three's a crowd. Hit the hay early, Paula. It'll help. As for you, Mr. Barnes, maybe I'll ring your place later. S'long.'

Bill Hatch was like that. Gone before you'd hardly grasped the fact that he was leaving. I had some of my drink, and suddenly didn't want any more. Two couples we both knew vaguely had come into the lounge. I wasn't in the mood for company, and I knew that Paula wasn't either.

'How about getting your room, sending for your bag, and then going over to that place on Tenth to eat?' I said quickly to Paula.

She caught the faint movement of my head, saw two couples threading tables in our general direction, and got up at once. 'Let's,' she said, and grabbed for her purse. 'What I want least of tonight is people. Come on.'

I tossed a bill on the table to cover everything for Nick, and followed her out the side entrance and back to the lobby. While Paula registered for a room, I went to the manager and got a manila envelope. I put the twenty-five thousand in it, sealed it, and signed my name across the face. The manager gave me a receipt and put the envelope in the safe. I went over and joined Paula. She had registered, and out the corner of my eye I saw somebody else we both knew fighting her way through the lobby crowd to greet us. I hooked my arm in Paula's and steered her fast out the Vanderbilt Avenue entrance. A cab was right there, and we popped into it. The cabby was tooling away just as a shrill voice called Paula's name from the entrance. We both held our eyes front, and our cab kept right on going.

'Damn that louse who got himself murdered in my bed, Gerry!' Paula breathed fiercely. 'We've got to solve this crazy business, if it's the last thing we do!'

I put my arm around her and pulled her close. 'We is right,' I said. 'And we will!'

And I crossed all the fingers of my other hand as I said it.

8

Dinner at one of our little off-the-beaten track favorite restaurants was a somber and silent affair for Paula and me. And I was more or less responsible. Every time she started a conversation about the day's doings, I either switched topics, or urged her to eat and then we'd talk later.

And for two reasons. One, because I felt sure that food would help her case of jim-jams. And second, because I wanted to do a little thinking on my own — undisturbed. So I did. About everything in general, and then three items in particular. Reading from left to right, they were — a persistent feeling that I had missed something in Paula's apartment. I mean, a spoken word, an action, or an object. For the life of me I couldn't pin it down. The other — why had White, whom I had believed a cripple, been spying on me, and had it really been White? And the last — had Paula and I been followed to the restaurant? I had had the feeling that we were being followed all the way. But it was dark, and maybe the same pair of taxi lights hadn't made every turn we had.

Anyway, I did a lot of heavy thinking about those three items. But I must confess that by the time Persian coffee and a pony of brandy were placed in front of me, I was still doing little more than thinking in circles. A moment later Paula got my attention, and held it.

'Gerry, I'm all sixes and sevens, and desperately tired. You do want me to have a good night's rest tonight, don't you?'

'You're darn tooting!' I said, and crooked a finger for the check. 'Down that stuff and I'll take you back to the hotel. I'm sorry, honey, but I thought this dinner — '

'Oh, it has, really!' she broke in, and smiled across at me. 'That's not what I mean. Please tell me all about it, Gerry. Your gal Friday. Remember?'

I remembered, and suddenly felt a little tired myself. It seemed a thousand years back to that morning in my office. 'I've been intending to tell you all along. But not until we were alone, because . . . Well, because it's all so screwy.'

'How screwy?' she kept after me. 'Tell me.'

So I did, but with a slight soft-pedaling of the kicking around I received from Jake. Paula listened, wide-eyed and open-mouthed, right to the end.

'Well, of all things!' was her first comment. 'Screwy is right! And you're sure you really saw this White hovering around the lounge?'

'If it wasn't, then he's got a twin brother,' I said doggedly. 'Look, Paula. In your apartment . . . something wasn't right. I can't think, and it's driving me nuts.'

'My apartment?' she echoed, and puckered her fine brows. 'What do you mean?'

'I don't know,' I sighed. 'But something about your apartment is trying to bust through into the old brain, but it just won't.'

She looked at me steady-eyed, but with a warmth in the depths that certainly drew me to the gal.

'I think you'd better turn in too, Gerry,' she said quietly. 'And put something on that bump. It's turning a hideous blue. Does it hurt much?'

'Something terrible,' I said. 'But I can wait until we're in the taxi. Come on.'

On the way back to the Biltmore I spent most of my time getting a nice crick in my neck from looking out the rear window. And I was just as uncertain as I was certain that we were being followed by the time the cab pulled up to the Biltmore marquee. I paid off, took Paula inside, and collected her room key. The lad at the desk said her bag had arrived and been sent up. I thanked him, and rode up with her. The floor lady on duty watched me like a hawk, ready to yell if I went in. I didn't. I unlocked the door and pushed it open.

'Good night, lovely,' I said, and kissed her. 'Get oodles and oodles of sleep. Tomorrow is another day, as they say.'

'And you too, Gerry,' she said, and gave me all the warmth in her eyes. 'You're going right home, aren't you?'

'Yes, by way of Centre Street,' I told her. 'I want to see Bierman and have a talk. After all . . . ' I stopped it there, and gestured.

'Of course, darling,' she said. 'Absolutely Bierman. But let's have breakfast together, shall we?'

'A date.' I nodded. Then, 'Shall I phone, or just nudge you?'

'Three guesses,' she said, and with a soft laugh closed the door in my face.

I said a polite good-night to the female floor warden and took the elevator down. Out in front, I grabbed a cab and told the lad to take me to Centre Street Headquarters. He was waiting for the red to go green at Forty-second Street when I changed my mind. I suddenly thought I had pinned down the elusive thought concerning Paula's apartment. I remembered Rita Rollins telling me about her Club Royale singing contract. And I remembered, too, that White had said he'd called the unknown Jordan at the Club Royale.

My once firm decision to bank the twenty-five grand and let White and his gorillas whistle sort of evaporated. I decided to do some work on the White case before going on down to Centre Street. So I had the cabby stop at the first drugstore while I checked with the phone directory. Rita's Twelfth Street address and phone number were the same as two years ago. I took out a nickel, lifted it halfway to the coin slot, and then put it back into my pocket. I might change my mind again on the way. Besides, Rita got a kick out of my surprise visits. Or used to.

As an example of how things happening fast can make you forget other things, I had paid off the cabby in front of Rita's five-story housekeeping apartment building and sent him on his way, when the light suddenly dawned. Rita at the moment no doubt was singing and swinging at Teddy Dane's Inn up the Albany Post Road. However, in view of the fact that Paula and I had not shown up as promised, perhaps the party had busted up and returned to town. Anyway, I could at least find out.

So I went up the steps and through the

door into the dimmed-out vestibule. I was looking over the apartment bell-button cards for Rita's name, when the inner door slammed open and a one-man tank charge went by me. He was swearing a lot of familiar words we coined and used in the Southwest Pacific whenever the Nips, or High Brass, made things difficult for us. In a nostalgic moment I almost called out to him just to find out what outfit he had been with, and just where. I even took a couple of steps after him, but I checked both voice and movements as I saw him pass under the street light just outside. The lad was a Naval Aviation j.g. And what's more, he was Harry Trent, Rita's latest flame with money in his pockets.

I watched Trent speed down to the corner and fling himself into a cab. When the cab whirled away I went back into the foyer, found Rita's card button and jabbed it. The inner door latch clicked. I went through and up to the third-floor rear, trying not to think that it was just like old-home week.

The lady answered my ring almost

instantly, and her dark eyes were full of hornet glares, and her ruby lips were parted to scream the works at me. She didn't. A flash change to wild joy spread over her face, and in the next half-second I had been physically yanked into the apartment and was fighting for my life. Or for air, anyway.

'Gerry, darling! Oh, this *is* wonderful!'

There was more that I didn't get, or even try to listen to. I held her off at a safe distance.

'Hold it, baby. I break easy. Remember? Frankly, I just dropped by to apologize for not showing up at your little celebration.'

She pouted and looked hurt at that one. Then with a smile she whirled around, showing lots of curved white leg under her swishing hostess gown, and went across the room and mixed two drinks. She came back, flounced down on the couch, and touched the bottom of my glass to the cushion beside her.

'We'll celebrate right here and now, darling,' she purred. 'Come to mama, Gerry.'

I could do with a drink, so I went over and sat down beside her. The lady robbed me of a sip before she handed me my drink. I grinned and rotated the glass until the lipstick marks were clear, and took a long pull. Then I leaned back and let her snuggle a little.

'What was the boyfriend mad about?' I asked casually.

She started a little, and pushed away so that she could look at me. 'You met Harry?'

'No. He went by too fast. But I heard him. He sounded like an unhappy guy. What's the matter? Did he run out of money?'

'You can be a bastard, can't you, Gerry?' she said calmly. 'I sometimes wish I'd never met you. That was the only thing you disliked in me, wasn't it? Well, I can't help it. I do like money. With all I've got, I should have been born to money. I wasn't! My family was . . . Oh, skip it!'

'Was I arguing?' I murmured.

She looked up at me, and damned if there wasn't the shadow of tears in her eyes. 'But with you, Gerry, it wasn't money,' she said in a broken whisper. 'I know . . . you thought so. But it wasn't really, darling. I . . . Oh, Gerry!'

I let her weep on my manly chest because, frankly, I was just a little surprised. I had lived through all of Rita's one thousand and one moods in years gone by. But this was mood one thousand and two. After a spell I chucked up her chin and kissed her.

'Don't be like that,' I said gently. 'You're swell, baby. And we had lots of fun, didn't we?'

She dried her tears by having a long drink, and when she smiled at me the mood was gone. 'Damn right, we did!' she said. 'And if only . . . Can you blame me for hating Paula's guts? If it hadn't been for her, why maybe . . . '

'Nuts!' I cut in, because the conversation was going up the wrong road. 'Don't be like that, either. In the old days, you and Paula used to be tops with each other. And you're still tops with her. So cut out — '

Her lips stopped me. Or maybe I let them stop me. 'I'm sorry, Gerry,' she whispered. 'I'm a perfect bitch. Particularly when Paula's in such a jam. She didn't murder him, really, did she?'

'What? How did you know . . . about Paula?'

'The evening paper, damn you.' She nodded at the table.

I glanced at the paper on the table. It wasn't a banner headline, but it was big enough. 'Mystery Killing on Swank East Side,' it read. I silently cursed all police reporters and newspaper copy desk men, and leaned over and picked up the paper. The story didn't take up even a stick of type. It didn't say any more than that Paula had found an unknown man murdered in her apartment. But that was more than enough, the way I was feeling. Then I got sense and cooled off. I drained my drink and handed Rita my glass.

'Two more, and I'm sorry, sweet,' I said. 'I've had a tough day. Forgive, huh?'

She debated a moment whether to let me have my empty glass over the head. And then kissed me. 'You're such a goddam heel, Gerry,' she said, getting up. 'But I love you so, dammit.'

I sat glaring at the newspaper while she made the drinks. She came back with them in another mood. Serious-eyed and sympathetic.

'That's why you shooed us out, Gerry? And you did, you know. It — I mean he was there all the time? Poor Paula! By the way, where is she now? I phoned but there wasn't any answer.'

'Staying with friends, and she's all right,' I said. 'Yeah, that's why I threw you out. It's a mess.'

'But you'll solve it, darling,' she said against me. 'I just know you will. And if there's anything, darling . . . But I don't suppose there would be, would there?'

I shrugged, and had a drink. Talk of the unknown murder had thrown me off course. That wasn't why I had dropped in to see Rita. I had another pull on the scotch and leaned back. 'It'll be a cinch,' I said, and squeezed her. 'But about the boyfriend. Why was he sore?'

'Why do men who get sent home get sore?' she countered.

I let that one ride for what it was worth. 'Struck me as not a bad guy,' I grunted.

'Where did you meet him, anyway?'

'Club Royale. He was one of a bunch there with Beth Price. He caught my eye, and Beth didn't seem to mind. That was that. But you'd better watch out, Gerry.'

'Huh? Me?'

'No,' she said. 'Paula. Harry, the louse, is that way about Paula. I can tell. When you two didn't show up, he was the one all for coming back to town. Personally, I don't go for him enough to care a damn. It really is still you, darling.'

A couple of minutes later, I put the question to her as casually as I could. 'Ever meet a navy flier at the club by the name of Jordan?'

'Why, yes, sure!' she said, brightening. 'A swell egg. He . . . No, wait a minute. Perry Jordan wasn't a navy pilot. He was infantry.'

'This lad was navy,' I said. 'Pal of mine. Heard he was in town recently, and the Royale was always his hangout. Maybe Trent knows him.'

'Well, you could ask Harry,' Rita said. Then with a wicked little smile, 'Or Paula could. Harry's a neighbor of hers. Or didn't you know?'

I sat up before I could stop myself.

'Come again?'

'Sure,' she said, and loved it. 'Harry has an apartment in the same building. Been there almost a month now. Not the swank kind that Paula has, though.'

I chuckled to cover up for a whole lot of fast and furious thoughts I was getting about then.

'No soap, sweet,' I said. 'This is one guy not worrying about one guy named Trent. Besides, remember what I used to say? I'm keeping bachelor quarters until I'm a hundred? By then I should know all there is to know.'

'A date,' she said, and maybe the scotch was making her voice a little too high. 'And then I'll show you lots of things you *don't* know!'

She leaned toward me to maybe give me a sample, but I suddenly wanted out. The social call was over as far as I was concerned. Besides, I could hear thunder booming over on the Jersey side. I finished my drink, gave Rita a peck on the cheek, and pushed myself up.

'Gotta get some sleep, beautiful,' I said, and reached for my hat. 'You, too. Thanks for the liquor.'

She got up fast, all hurt and angry. 'But, darling, why bother?' she cried. 'Don't be a stick. Besides, there's a thunderstorm coming up, and you'll probably never get a taxi at this hour.'

I backed to the door, shaking my head. 'No dice, lovely,' I said. Then, because maybe I am that kind of a heel on occasion, I added with a grin, 'Anyway, I'm fresh out of mink coats. And really tired. S'long.'

'You no-good bum, Gerry Barnes!'

I shut the door fast. Going down the front steps, I pulled out my handkerchief and wiped Rita's lipstick off. And then suddenly lightning, but not of the storm coming up, struck with a bang inside the old head.

I stood there, open-mouthed, like a stone statue. 'My God!' I choked out hoarsely. And repeated, 'My God!'

A night owl passing by at the moment shot me a scared look, and hurried up his pace.

9

Lieutenant Frank Bierman of homicide looked slightly surprised, and equally annoyed, when I walked into his office. But the smile he presently gave me, and the gesture, were polite enough.

'Come in, Barnes, and sit down. How did you leave Miss Grant?'

'Sleepy,' I said, and sat down and accepted the cigarette he offered. And when we were both puffing, 'Found out anything interesting?'

'Nothing,' he said, and his face sobered. 'Death was at a few minutes after ten o'clock. And it was from the knife. According to Sperry, another six months and alcohol would have done the same thing for him. He was plastered when he was murdered.'

'I noticed the telltale marks,' I murmured. 'Any idea who he is?'

'Not yet,' Bierman said. 'Nobody wanted by the police. We haven't his fingerprints on file. Frankly, it's rather an odd killing.'

'How so?' I prodded.

'Appearances don't actually tell you much,' he said, playing with a pencil. 'But from his general looks, and the kind of clothes he wore, I wouldn't say he was the kind to be found in Miss Grant's apartment.'

'And just what do you mean by that?' I demanded, starting to get sore.

'Not at all what you're thinking, Barnes,' he rebuffed me quietly. 'I simply mean that he didn't belong any place in that building. Some place on Broadway, or even Lexington, yes. But definitely not in the section where we found him.'

'How about identification marks?' I asked to keep the conversation going. 'Did Doctor Sperry find any?'

The quick look he gave me made it plain enough that I had struck oil. 'What makes you ask that, Barnes?'

'Just curious,' I replied. 'Why? Were there?'

'Whether it's an identification mark or not, we don't know yet,' he said. 'But on his left upper arm is some tattooing. Faded, but readable under a glass. Three initials and a number — T, B, F, and the number ten. The initials probably stand for his name, but I haven't the faintest what the number means. Maybe he was ten years old when he had it done.'

Little stabs of high voltage were shooting through me, but I held hard onto myself and shrugged as I pulled on my cigarette. 'Could be,' I murmured. Then, with a half laugh, 'Now, all you have to do is find out what names the initials represent.'

'Part of the job, yes,' Bierman murmured. Then, giving me a faint smile, 'You've taken this case, of course? In Miss Grant's interests?'

I nodded and waited. And not for long, either.

'Well, I hope you'll cooperate with us, Barnes,' he said. 'Believe me, it'll work out best that way for everybody concerned.'

Once again, I couldn't tell whether it was advice or a threat. I decided to find out.

'You mean you really think Miss Grant's involved?' I said. I guess I must have shown something in my face. Bierman smiled. Almost paternally.

'Keep your shirt on, Barnes,' he said. 'You both are involved until you're un-involved, to coin a word. But neither of you need lose much sleep over it.'

'Thanks,' I said, and tried to make my voice dry. Then, as a thought came, 'What about the knife? Any prints on it?'

'Wiped clean as a whistle,' he said with a little hard laugh. 'But even a ten-year-old would know enough to do that. Well, anything else, Barnes?'

I can take a hint, so I shook my head and stood up. Then I turned to him and put a half-sheepish grin on my face. 'I've done quite a bit of homework on fingerprinting,' I said. 'Any chance of your giving me a copy of his?'

'Why?' The word came at me like a bullet.

'My first case,' I said with a laugh. 'Souvenir, if you like. Anyway, will you?'

Bierman scowled, chewed on his lower lip — and looked at me and through me.

I waited for the 'No,' but it didn't come. 'Go to Room 642,' he said with a gesture. 'Tell Sergeant Clarke to give you a copy. I'll call him and tell him you'll be along to pick them up. And, Barnes!'

'Yes?' innocently.

'Bear in mind what I said. Cooperation will be much better for us all around. It's your first case, so be smart and don't make it the last as far as the friendship of this bureau is concerned. Good night, Barnes.'

I assured Bierman, and meant it, that I certainly wanted continued close friendship with the police department. Then I left him, went down to Room 642 and picked up a copy of the dead man's prints. From there, I went out to the street in search of a cab. It was close to the bewitching hour of midnight by then and the Barnes was really approaching the all-in stage.

Well, in due time a night cruiser came along. I flagged it and rode it to my apartment in the east seventies. A nice place, but not as gold braid and swanky as the apartment where Paula pays rent.

Even though that dear departed uncle had left me enough of the wherewithal to pay the limit I had selected slightly more modest diggings, because I like the simple things. Except in women!

Be that as it may, however, as I paid off the cabby and was turning to head in through the doors a long black Caddy slid silently by. There was plenty of other traffic, too, so it was only by chance that I happened to spot the Caddy. And when I did, I froze and watched it disappear up the street. Yes, I had had a couple of rides in that same car during the day. And to see it slide by in front of my place struck me as being considerably more than mere coincidence. Exactly! I was ready to give you any odds you wanted that one Mr. White had made sure of my every movement ever since our unusual meeting. But *why* was something else again.

Most of the pleasant feeling my visit to Bierman's office had brought me slid away in thin air as I stood there on the sidewalk staring in the direction the Caddy had taken. Presently, though, I snapped out of it and went inside and up to my quarters. My first act, after peeling to the belt line for comfort, was a drink. Then I took pen and paper and wrote a letter to a close pal of mine in the navy department in Washington. I addressed the envelope, put the letter, and the copy of the dead lad's prints, inside, sealed it, and marked it air mail.

Lounging back comfortably in my best easy chair, I began with the first event of the day and reviewed them all in detail up to the present moment. Some of it made me grin, some of it made me frown and scratch the old head, and some of it made me pretty sore. Then on impulse I got the phone directory and started checking the White listings, looking for ones in the Ninety-sixth and West End Avenue area. The nearest I could get to that area was on Riverside Drive and Eighty-fourth. So I gave up. Either an unlisted phone, or maybe White had told the truth about not having one around his place. Or, maybe White wasn't his name?

Thought of that last gave me food for more thinking, but I didn't get anywhere. Sleep was really pulling at the eyelids by then, and the brain was bushed as regards trying to make sense out of anything. So I went into the bedroom that looks out on the street, and started to reach for the light switch. On a sudden hunch I dropped my hand and went over to one of the windows and looked out.

Pay dirt, first look! Jake was across the street and a couple of buildings up from mine. His size alone could have told me that, but I knew for sure it was Jake because of the way he sort of held his head a little to the right, as though his left ear was the best for hearing.

Yes, there he was. On White's orders, no doubt, standing guard on me, or, anyway, the place where I lived. Why? I couldn't even guess, and I didn't bother. I was too busy getting sore at White for this crazy shadowing business. And sorer and sorer at Jake for the tossing-around he'd given me.

'Okay, so what can you do about it?' I grunted at myself aloud.

And as though in answer to my question, the invisible gremlins tipped me off to a swell idea! I went back into the living room and gathered up the clothes I had peeled off. Then back to the bedroom, switching on the light this time. Standing close enough to the window so that Jake could see me from below across the street, I put on my clothes and went through all the motions of getting ready to go out. Then I moved away from the window, left the light on, and went out of the apartment. I took the self-operating night elevator clear down to the basement. The janitor, half asleep, opened one eye long enough to recognize me, and then went back to sleep.

I went out the basement side door to an alley that slanted up to the sidewalk and street. It was where they parked the ashcans and such for every other day collection. As luck would have it for me, there were half a dozen full to the brim. Keeping in the dark shadow cast by the building, I moved four of them as close to the front of the building as I could, and put them in line straight out from the building wall. Then, after taking a quick peek around the corner to note that Jake was still standing his post, I skipped back through the basement door and on up to my apartment.

Once more in the bedroom, and close to the windows, I put on my hat and brushed a few invisible specks of dust off my jacket. Then, switching out all the lights, I took the elevator down to the lobby floor, and on out to the sidewalk. There Jake still stood across the street and a couple of buildings up. I gave him just a flash glance, but I could almost hear his bones creak when he stiffened at the sight of me!

Hands in my pockets, I walked along to the right for maybe fifty steps. Then I spun around and sprinted back along the sidewalk. When I reached the alley I swerved in sharply, breathed a prayer that my hurdling skill in school years ago had not left me, and left the cement. It hadn't, and I cleared those rubbish cans in what I like to think was faultless style, and continued on down to the basement side door. I popped in, closed the door to within a couple of inches, and waited.

Joy of joys for me! Jake's footsteps came pounding. Then he in person came barging around the corner of the building. Too late, he let out a strangled yell. He hit that row of four rubbish cans under a full head of steam. The noise that followed was enough to wake the dead. But the clash and clang of those cans, and the choice words that poured from Jake's throat, constituted sweet music to my ears.

I waited until it had died to muffled moans and groans, and then went back up to the apartment, undressed in the dark and slid into bed still puzzled, still sore in a lot of places, but terribly pleased in a strictly malicious sort of way!

10

The first thing that registered on the waking brain the next morning was the insistent ringing of the telephone. Still drugged with sleep, I cursed it, rolled over, and then sat up straight in bed as memories came flooding back. The table clock told me it was eight-thirty, and that sent me out of bed fast and over to the phone. My breakfast date with Paula, of course! I got the thing out of its cradle in a hurry.

'Beat me by half a second, darling!' I said as cheerily as I could make the voice. 'Just calling you when you rang.'

My error! It wasn't Paula.

'Gerry!' came Rita's voice over the wire, high and slightly out of control. 'Come down right away, will you? You must!'

'Down where?' I wanted to know. 'What's the matter?'

'My place,' she told me. 'I'll tell you

when you get here, not now. Please, darling. It's terribly, terribly important!'

Experience had taught me not to trust Rita. Particularly that early in the morning.

'You have a nightmare or something?'

'Don't be like that!' she screamed at me. 'Please, Gerry, or . . . or I don't know what will happen. I . . . Oh, Gerry, if you ever loved me even a little, please come right away!'

'Now look, Rita — ' I said, but that's as far as I got. The receiver clicked in my ear as she hung up.

I said nuts to her, and took a quick shower and shave. When I was in my clothes, I went to the phone to call Paula. But I dialed Rita's number instead. No answer. I spent about five seconds telling myself that it was just another one of Rita's crazy come-on gags. That the gal just wouldn't realize that Paula was way out in front.

But that didn't work. I got to thinking about the way her voice had sounded, and that got me to worrying. Or maybe it just got me too curious for my peace of mind.

Anyway, I grabbed up my hat, and the air-mail letter to my navy department friend in Washington, and went down and out into the morning sunlight. I dropped the letter in the corner box, and hailed a cab.

When I jabbed Rita's foyer bell button, I had to wait a couple of minutes before the clicking came. I went in and up to the third floor rear. Her door was open an inch or two, so I didn't bother to ring. I just knocked and pushed on in.

'Listen, beautiful, what's the big — '

At that precise instant the roof fell in and hit me on the back of the head, dead center between the ears. For a flash instant I saw all the colored stars imaginable, and a half million zinging comets. Then I fell down a great big black hole, landed on a soft billowy cloud, and went floating away on it into complete oblivion.

When I came to, I was flat on my back staring up at a ceiling that was painted shell-pink. It seemed to hurt my eyes, and so I closed them and tried to go back to sleep, but I couldn't because a thousand little demons with steam shovels were excavating the back half of my skull. I managed to roll over and push up onto my hands and knees. And there I stayed for a spell, hanging onto nothing while the room went around and around.

Eventually, when I was fairly sure that my head wasn't going to drop off, I got to my feet and hung onto a chair for support. Then, using one eye at a time, I looked around. My first thought was that I was back in the London blitz and that a blast from a near miss had done its stuff. But when I saw, and realized, that all the glass was still in the windows, I caught on that such was not the case. Rita's place had been turned upside down not from the outside, but from the inside. Table drawers, desk drawers, closets and what-not had been emptied out, the contents all on the floor.

Groggy-eyed, I stared at the mess, trying to work up even a half guess. But the little demons wouldn't let me. So I staggered into the bathroom and stuck my head under the cold water tap. The first shock almost passed me out, but I managed to hang on, and gradually the little demons started to take time off. After toweling my head around and over the bump, I went out into the living room and straight to Rita's liquor cabinet. Praise Allah, its contents had not been disturbed. Two quick straight ones, and I made up my mind to go on living for a little while, anyway.

And then I really started to take stock of things. The apartment was made up of bedroom, living room, bath, kitchenette, and a postage-stamp-sized dining alcove. I went slowly through all of them, and all of the rooms were a mess. Perhaps the bedroom most, because Rita was always more than nuts about clothes, and had enough stuff to outfit a dozen women. There were even ten pair of nylons tossed about, so of course I knew right then and there that no member of the fair sex had gone through in high gear.

Well, at the end of the tour the buzzing and clanking brain arrived at the logical, not to say obvious, conclusion. Somebody had been looking for something in Rita's apartment. And had found it, or hadn't found it. My arrival, of course, had been during the search. And the searcher had employed a most effective method to prevent my bothering him any. All that decided for myself, I had some more of Rita's scotch, sat down in a chair that was still on its four legs, and tried to do some thinking.

It just wasn't my morning for thinking. Why Rita had wanted me, I didn't know. Why she hadn't waited for me, I didn't know. Who had torn the place apart, and clouted me, I didn't know either. In short, I didn't know anything, except that my watch said quarter of ten, and that Paula was probably brewing up a beautiful mad on me.

So I got up, took a glance at the phone and decided no, and went out and down to the street. The sunlight hit me hard, and I had to halt for a couple of minutes to get all parts of me organized. Then I started walking toward the corner in search of a cab. I was halfway there when a voice stopped me.

'Oh, Mr. Barnes, please!'

I stopped, turned around, and there

was Kirby of the rat eyes. I blinked at his polite smile as he walked up, and then looked past him at the Caddy parked at the curb. Mike, not Jake, was behind the wheel. I was happy for a brief instant, picturing Jake in the hospital with two broken legs!

Kirby's smile faded when he got close and took a good look at me. It changed to an expression of concern. That fell flat as far as I was concerned.

'Are you ill, Mr. Barnes? You don't look well.'

'I'm okay,' I cut him off, and fixed my eyes on the Caddy. 'What do you want, Kirby?'

His charming cobra smile came back. 'Why, nothing, personally,' he said. 'I just happened to see you, and . . . er . . . Mr. White would like to talk with you.'

The fact that Kirby's hand was in his right jacket pocket wasn't lost on me at all. I ignored it and looked him in the eye, and wondered crazily if that gun in his pocket had made contact with my head a while back. It did seem truly screwy on second thought, so I brushed it aside.

'Does he?' I grunted. 'What about?'

Kirby shrugged his padded shoulders and sweetened his smile. 'I really don't know,' he said. 'He gave me orders to find you. I phoned, but you did not answer your phone. I was on my way back when I happened to see you come out of a building back there.'

My respect for Kirby went way down below nil. Maybe he was a smooth lad in some things, but he certainly was one of the world's lousiest liars. Back to Ninety-sixth via Twelfth Street? Horses!

'Try again, Kirby!' I snapped. 'And by the way, I don't like people following me around. How's your ape friend, Jake?'

'As well as could be expected, Mr. Barnes,' he said, and his grin was almost friendly. 'What did happen, anyway? Jake swore that it was a truck.'

'That's right, a truck.' I grinned back at him. 'Jake went to sleep watching my place, and fell off the curb. White would do better hiring midgets.'

Kirby thought that was quite funny. With his lips, but not with his eyes.

'Oh, Jake and Mike have their uses, Mr.

Barnes,' he chuckled. Then, letting it die out, 'But now that I've found you, let's — '

'Save it,' I stopped him. 'I'm late for an appointment now. Give me White's phone number. I'll call him later. Matter of fact, I want to talk to him, too.'

'I'm sure he won't keep you long,' came the smooth voice. 'Besides, Mr. White has no phone. Truly, it'll only be a few minutes.'

'Nuts!' I said, getting sore. 'White just hired me for a certain job. He doesn't own me. You run back and tell him that!'

I started to turn, but he moved quickly and I felt the muzzle of his gun digging into my hip.

'Don't be that way, Barnes,' he growled, the polish all gone. 'White wants to see you, and so you're going to see White! Let's go!'

My own gun in my shoulder holster was doing me a lot of good. Maybe Kirby was bluffing there on the sidewalk in broad daylight. But a look into those mean eyes of his didn't make me think so. Besides, I couldn't see a single soul on either side of the street. But I could see Mike starting to open the Caddy door.

'The answer is — no!' I snapped at Kirby, as mounting anger pushed common sense over the brink. 'So what are you going to do about it?'

For maybe two seconds Kirby's wicked eyes locked with mine. Then a funny expression came over his face. And at about that same instant a hand slapped my back, and a voice spoke in my ear.

'Well, well, pal Barnes, damned if not! Been looking all over for you, pal, and have you got a drink? Well, you going to introduce me to your friend, huh?'

It was Bill Hatch, and seventeen sheets to the wind. He hung onto me, and I had to brace so he wouldn't pull me over. I felt like kissing him, I was that glad.

'Hi, Bill!' I said, and pulled away from Kirby. 'Boy, have you tied one on. Kirby, meet Hatch of the *Globe*.'

'Hi, Kirby!' Bill mumbled, and pawed the air in salute. 'You got a drink on you, huh?'

Kirby's eyes glittered, but he managed a smile. 'Sorry, but I haven't,' he said.

Then, with a glance my way, 'Nice to have met you, Barnes. I'll pick you up later. And I really will. S'long.'

''Bye,' I said. 'My love to Jake, Kirby.'

If he heard he paid no attention. He went back to the Caddy and got in. Mike rolled the Caddy past us, Bill hanging onto me to keep from falling down. We both watched it go to the end of the street, make the corner and disappear. I took hold of Hatch's arms to steady him.

'God bless you, you potted bum!' I said. 'But where in — '

I got that far and stopped short. Bill's drunken pose had gone away in nothing flat. He was standing in front of me as sober as I was. Grinning quizzically, and one eyebrow cocked.

'I seem to have missed a few chapters, my friend,' he said. 'What's the story all about now? Why did that hood have a gun on you?'

'He wanted me to ride in his Caddy,' I said. 'But just how did you happen to come along?'

'Following you,' he said. 'On my way to your place when you came out in a rush.

Followed your cab down here but lost it. Then the Hatch brain remembered that Rita lives down this way. Hunting for her address when I saw the lad trying to convince you of something. I just couldn't wait to find out what. So?'

'I'm not sure myself, but thanks, pal,' I said, and started walking. 'Got to beat it up to see Paula. I haven't even called her yet, and — '

'And you are in the dog house, really!' Bill cut in. 'I phoned her a while back, and the things she called you before I could stop her long enough to say it was me! The woman is really annoyed, Gerry.'

I imagined so, and I wondered if I hadn't better do a couple of things I intended doing, and give Paula time to cool off. But I decided, no, because Paula isn't the type that cools off until she's damn good and ready. Such as when she has you on bended knee, your head bowed and bloodied, so to speak.

'Thanks for the tip,' I said, quickening my pace. 'I think I'll try a dozen roses this time. Outside of being sore at me, was she okay?'

Bill didn't reply. He whistled at an approaching cab before I could so much as purse my lips. The cab swung into the curb, brakes screaming. Bill opened the door and thumbed me in. He pushed in after me and yanked the door shut.

'The Biltmore, bud,' he said, and settled back. Then, cocking his head my way, 'So you won't talk to a guy who saves your life, huh?'

'About what?' I grunted, and wished I had a pocket flask on me to help the back of my head.

'Several things, chum,' Bill said in a quiet, serious tone. 'Yesterday it was just a simple unexplained murder. Today it's you tearing around in high gear, and hoods holding guns on you. I don't quite follow.'

'Neither do I,' I said, and meant it. 'When I do I'll tell you. Right now, shut up and let me get in the mood to combat Paula.'

Bill took the hint for about half a minute.

'I saw Bierman early this morning, Gerry.'

'Yeah?'

'Yeah. He hasn't identified friend stiff yet, but says he will before the day's out. He told me to thank you if and when I saw you.'

'How's that?' I barked. 'What does he mean? I don't get it.'

'Neither do I.' He grinned. 'When I do I'll tell you.'

I started a hot retort, but let it go because I couldn't be bothered. Instead I leaned back on the cab cushions and tried to reason out for myself why Bierman wanted to thank me for something, and what.

I was still trying to figure when the cab pulled up at the Biltmore. Then I stopped trying to figure and got mad some more as I recognized a plain-clothesman from Centre Street leaning nonchalantly against the fender of a cab parked a few yards down from the entrance.

11

I waited until I paid off the Cabby before I spoke. 'Bierman, the trusting soul!' I growled out the corner of my mouth. 'What's he think Paula's going to do, anyway?'

Hatch followed my look and grunted. 'There's a lot of crime on the police blotter,' he said. 'Maybe it isn't Paula. Let's go find her. I could enjoy some fireworks.'

He was inside and going up the wide stairs to the lobby before I caught up with him.

'Paula's my gal; scram,' I said. Then, as he started to open his mouth, 'Go on, will you? I'll meet you in the men's bar in just a few minutes.'

I thought for a moment he was still going to protest. But instead, he suddenly grinned and nodded. 'A deal,' he said. 'I can't stand bloodshed, anyway.'

I heaved a sigh of relief and went over

to the desk and picked up one of the house phones. The lad on duty recognized me, and guessed correctly. 'Miss Grant is in the breakfast room, Mr. Barnes,' he told me.

I thanked him, and went over. Angelo was on duty and greeted me, all smiles. Then let them quickly fade as he leaned toward me slightly.

'Miss Grant is at the corner table there, Mr. Barnes,' he said with a half-nod of his head. 'She does not feel good this morning. But who can blame her, eh? It must have been a terrible experience. I feel so sorry for her.'

'You can start feeling a little sorry for me, too, Angelo,' I grunted as Paula turned her head at that moment and spotted me.

'Sorry for you, Mr. Barnes?'

I left Angelo's question hanging in the air, and threaded the tables over to the corner. Paula was looking out the window, but the set of her chin was warning enough. The ashtray held half a dozen stubs, and I could tell that her cup of coffee was stone cold. I slid into the chair across from her.

'Sorry, darling,' I said. 'The light of your life overslept.'

'Liar!' she said without turning her head. 'Your phone rang enough times to wake ten men.'

'Okay, okay, I'm still sorry, honest,' I tried to mollify her. 'I was delayed. Rita phoned me, and — '

'*Rita!*'

My, my, how the lightning flashed as her head came around. And it made me sore, I don't know why.

'Look, if you'd like me to leave, say so!' I growled. 'I'm trying to — '

'Don't be an ass! You're making a scene. What about your precious Rita?'

'*This* about my precious Rita,' I said. And then before she could think up another one, I told her the story of what had happened. 'And why I tell you, I don't know!' I finished up. 'You certainly don't rate it, the greeting I got!'

I made the play for a smile and a tender word about my poor head. I got thrown out halfway to first. Paula gave me a look and a sniff.

119

'A likely story!' she said. 'But if true, don't you know how to do anything but lead with your head? That's twice now.'

I burned so I couldn't speak. Then Angelo popped up to save one of us. He had a fresh pot of coffee and two clean cups and saucers. I grabbed the coffee and a cup and saucer, and waved the other away.

'Miss Grant's had enough, Angelo,' I said. 'Too late for eggs and bacon?'

Angelo gave us both a good look, then quickly assured me it wasn't too late and went away. Paula reached for the coffee but I pulled it out of her reach.

'Fattening,' I said. 'And you must be ten pounds over as it is.'

That held her, and I had some coffee. Then I looked at her killing me dozens of times with her eyes, and grinned.

'Silly, aren't we?' I said. 'We're supposed to be working together. Get any ideas in your dreams last night?'

'Yes,' she surprised me. Then, with rising anger, 'But if you think I'm going to tell — '

'Cut!' I stopped her. 'I'm sorry. I

apologize. But my head does hurt like hell. Here, have the damn coffee.'

She ignored the magnanimous gesture, glared at me for an instant or two more, and then let a little grin tug at the corners of her mouth. 'You need it, you look a sight,' she got in the last crack. Then, in a serious tone, 'But I did get something last night, Gerry. It was nearer morning, though. I woke up and couldn't get back to sleep. I got thinking about who in the world could have got hold of a key to the apartment.'

I stopped the coffee cup halfway to my face and put it down. There was a rippling tingle at the back of my neck. 'Yes? Who?'

'It was over a year ago,' she said. 'You were in China, and I was visiting Mother in Chicago. She asked if she could use my apartment while I was gone. Hers was being done over. I had two keys then, and gave her one. For the life of me, though, I can't remember whether she gave it back to me or not.'

'Who, your mother?' I asked weakly.

'Mother?' she echoed, startled. 'Of

course not! It was Beth Price. Didn't I say so?'

I didn't argue. Too much wind had been knocked out of my sails. Beth Price? Cute, sweet, but simple Beth Price had lured an unknown guy into Paula's apartment, and knifed him? It just didn't make sense. It didn't make sense at all. I could only gape at Paula.

'Certainly it's ridiculous!' she said, reading my thoughts, if any. 'But Beth did use my apartment, and I gave her a key. However . . . ' Paula paused, screwed up her lovely face, and gave a helpless shake of her head.

'Think hard,' I coaxed. 'Surely you can — '

'I can't!' she protested. 'But Beth, Gerry! She's one of my best friends. I just can't possibly imagine!'

Neither could I, but I just shrugged, and watched Angelo bringing my eggs and bacon.

'Remember anything else?' I asked when Angelo had gone. 'Such as when and where you met the dead guy?'

'No, that's definitely out,' Paula said.

'I'm positive, now, I never saw him before in my life. I just thought I had, that's all.'

And there the conversation went into a decline while I had my eggs and bacon and some more coffee.

'What about you?' Paula wanted to know as I wiped my mouth. 'Have your brains come up with anything besides bumps?'

'No,' I said, not quite truthfully. 'Right now, though, I want to find Rita. If you were Rita, where should I go looking for you?'

'I could answer that, but I'm a lady,' Paula said sweetly. 'Besides, nuts to Rita. You're supposed to be working for me, and *with* me, Mr. Detective!'

'Very funny,' I grunted, and reached for my wallet. 'But I'm still going to try and find her. It might be important. How about lunch? You do some more thinking about that key, and we'll compare notes. At the Colony, huh?'

'Sorry, darling, but I'm dated for lunch,' she said, practically drooling over each word.

'Yeah, who?'

'With a gentleman, darling,' she said. 'A gentleman who was kind enough to phone and see how I was this morning. A considerate and thoughtful gentleman.'

'Don't tell Bill Hatch you think he's a gentleman,' I laughed. 'He'd take it as an insult to his manhood. And right now he's in the men's bar, if you wish to join him. Which you can't!'

'Not Bill, though he's a dear to have called. Beloved, I'm having lunch with Clyde Mather. Do call me this evening, if it's okay with Rita. Bye-bye, darling!'

She was halfway to the door when the brains suddenly clicked, and I almost startled twenty or thirty people into a nice case of indigestion with my roar. 'Hey, wait a minute!'

Angelo had to pick up the breakfast check that morning because I clean forgot it in my haste to catch up with Paula. I did that in the lobby.

'I said wait!' I panted. 'Hold it!'

'You damn fool, are you mad?' she whispered furiously. 'What do you think I — '

'Shut up!' I pulled her over toward the

phone booths out of the path of goggling eyes. 'Look, did Clyde Mather call you here this morning? No kidding now!'

I could almost see a wisecrack sliding up out of her creamy white throat. But I guess my grip on her arm stopped it. She nodded.

'Yes, he did,' she said. 'And why shouldn't he have?'

'No reason,' I muttered while the brains groped out in all directions. 'No reason at all, except . . . how the hell did Mather know that you were stopping here? Answer me that one, Paula.'

She couldn't, and I watched the light dawn in her eyes. Then, being Paula, she promptly shrugged it off. 'I can't even guess, but I'll ask him at lunch.'

'Okay, okay!' I snapped when that was all I got for my fast thinking. 'Have a nice time. You, dear Mather, and the gumshoe.'

'Gumshoe! You mean . . . '

'Yes, my pet!' I said, and felt nasty, too. 'A guy was killed in your bedroom yesterday. Remember? And Bierman said last night we were both involved until he *un*-involved us. So have a nice time. Give my love to sweet Clyde . . . with arsenic in his teabag!'

And with that, I walked away from Paula. I had to scram before I said something that would really hurt. Just to think of that two-legged boll weevil, Mather, sitting across the luncheon table simpering, and undressing her eye by eye, got my cork for fair.

So I walked away, headed for the men's bar, and changed my mind. Instead, I went outside and took a taxi up to Paula's apartment building. Rita hadn't kidded me the night before.

Lieutenant Harry Trent's apartment was a couple of floors below Paula's. After I had found that out, I went up in the elevator unannounced. It was down the hallway to the left and at the end. I stabbed the bell button and waited.

Trent was in, and when he pulled open the door, the expression on his face changed about half a dozen times, and at lightning-like speed. For the first split second, his eyes were narrowed in smoldering rage, and his mouth was partly open as though he were going to give with a blast. In the next split second the expression was one of surprise from dimpled chin to hairline. And then caution, suspicion, and wariness had their turn. And finally, a sort of cold indifference.

'Hello.'

'Hello, Trent,' I said, and moved forward. 'Mind if I come in for a minute?'

If he did, and I thought so, there wasn't much he could do about it. I topped him by a couple of inches, and maybe fifteen pounds, so he stepped back and I was in. In, and getting a little surprise of my own. Seated in a chair over by the triple windows that looked out Long Island way was dear Clyde Mather no less. He had a drink in one hand and an eight-inch cigarette holder in the other. He seemed to be the least surprised of the two of us, because he spoke first.

'Why, hello, Gerry!' he gushed, but didn't get up. 'How's Paula?'

'Tops, thanks,' I grunted, and turned back to Trent, who stood by the door, sort of measuring me with his eyes, I thought.

'I didn't know you had company, Trent,' I said. 'Sorry.'

He walked a few steps and dropped into a chair. He picked up a drink and had some. 'Skip it,' he said, and waved a hand. 'Mix one if you want it. And what else do you want?'

I guess maybe I'm fussy, but I never accept a drink when it's offered that way. But I did sit down. 'I'm trying to locate Rita,' I said with a pleasant smile. 'Have you seen or heard from her this morning?'

Trent tried hard, but he just couldn't quite keep his face under control. His left cheek twitched three times in rapid succession. 'Why the hell should I?' he snapped.

I put my brows up in mild surprise. Inwardly I felt like pasting him one. 'Well, I don't know,' I said with a half-laugh. 'I just thought . . . well, you know.'

'Do I?' he countered, and regarded me steadily. Then, 'That was yesterday, Barnes. Today, that little floozy can drop dead for all I care.'

'Oh, I say, Harry!' That from Mather

over by the window, but we both ignored him.

'Rita is missing, Trent,' I said quietly. 'Could it have anything to do with the business last night?'

Trent looked a little startled. He put down his drink and sat up a little straighter. 'What business last night?' he demanded. 'What the hell do you mean?'

'Keep your shirt on, sailor!' I said, and gave him eye for eye. 'You had some kind of a battle with Rita last night, and blew in one hell of a huff. I'm interested.'

Maybe it was fear, or maybe anger, that blanched his face.

'You're crazy as hell, Barnes! Shove off!'

12

During the so-called pin-dropping silence that followed Trent's crack, I looked from him to Mather and thought what a real pleasure it would be to take on the two of them. Particularly so, Mather. A real pleasure indeed to spoil him for a certain luncheon date. And then I brushed aside my silly ideas and returned to the present.

'No, I'm not crazy, Trent,' I said. 'I saw you tear out of Rita's place. I was right in the vestibule, but you didn't see me. And Rita mentioned the fact that you two had had words.'

'So what?' was his comment.

'So nothing at all,' I said with a shrug. 'I'm simply wondering if it could have had anything to do with Rita's disappearance this morning. That's all.'

'It wouldn't,' Trent said sullenly. 'She just tried to play me for a sucker once too often. I don't know where she is, and I don't give a damn.'

I half-nodded, and then Mather spoke up. 'That would make you the last to have seen her, wouldn't it, Gerry?' he murmured. Then, with a cute little smile I longed to wipe off, 'Have you asked Paula? They used to be such dear friends, you know.'

I didn't miss the crack, but I ignored it. 'Paula hasn't heard from her,' I said. 'As for me being the last — maybe. She called me this morning to tell me something. I went down to get the rest of it, but she was gone.'

I don't know what caused me to tell them about Rita's phone call, but I did, and was instantly glad. Maybe psychic hunches come easy to fellows in my trade. Anyway it got them both. Way off guard, too. Trent spoke first.

'What did Rita have to tell you?' he demanded.

'Personal business,' I said. 'You know the business I'm in.'

'You mean Rita is in some trouble, Gerry?' Mather purred. 'And she has hired you?'

'Something like that,' I said with a wave

of my hand. Then, getting to my feet, 'Well, thanks for everything. If you do run into Rita tell her to call me, will you?'

'Yeah, sure,' Trent grunted, and didn't bother to get up.

I went through the half-motions of waving a goodbye salute, and then stopped it. I turned back to Trent. 'I meant to ask you yesterday when Rita introduced you,' I said. 'Were you on the same carrier as Torpedo Ten, Trent?'

He blinked a couple of times, and then shook his head. 'No. Ten was with the Third Fleet. Why?'

'A pal of mine was in Ten,' I said. 'I've lost track of him. Just wondered if you'd met up with him.'

I could have been wrong, but I think Trent's eyes narrowed. 'I knew a couple of fellows in Torpedo Ten,' he said slowly. 'What was his name?'

'Jordan,' I said. 'A. P. Jordan. Know him?'

Trent's eyes closed, and he furrowed his brows as though in deep thought. When he opened his eyes again, they were just two blank orbs. 'No, I never knew anybody by that name,' he said. 'S'long, Barnes.'

Being the touchy type, I resented the bum's rush technique. True, I could think of no reason to stick around with the pair of heels any longer. But my dander rose up and I promptly decided to stick around anyway. Maybe a little needling would hook together some of the daffy thoughts that were swimming around in the brain. Anyway, the annoyance that flashed in each face was worth the effort of reseating myself. I looked at Mather and smiled nicely.

'How did you find out Paula was at the Biltmore, Clyde?' I asked.

'Why, why do you ask, Gerry?' he said with his damn simpering laugh. 'Is that supposed to be connected with Rita's disappearance?'

'Maybe,' I grunted. 'Anyway, how did you find out?'

He made me wait until he'd stuck a cigarette into that eight inches of ivory and lighted up. 'A simple way, Gerry,' he said, smiling at me through the smoke. 'When I read about the distressing affair in her apartment, I phoned to give her what comfort I could. A policeman answered and referred me to Lieutenant Bierman. I called police headquarters and Bierman told me where Paula was spending the night. It was then too late to call the dear lady, so I waited until this morning. Incidentally, if you've seen her yourself this morning, then you know, eh?'

I was weak enough to let the smug smile burn me. And strong enough to smile right back at him just as smugly. 'The luncheon date?' I murmured. 'Why, certainly. Fact is, I insisted, when she wanted to break it. Luncheon with you will take her mind off the third party.'

Dear Clyde choked on a mouthful of smoke and had to go for his handkerchief. 'Third party?' he panted when he was all over coughing. 'Who? You?'

'No,' I said sadly. 'One of Bierman's men. Met him in the Biltmore lobby this morning. Crazy as it sounds, Paula is still on Bierman's doubt list.'

It gave me a bit of a jolt to see the indignant, righteous anger flame up in

Mather's face. I would never have believed he had that much red blood in his system.

'Paula a suspect?' he almost shouted. 'Why, of all the preposterous ideas! True, I know only what I've read in the papers. But I for one most certainly believe that Paula told the truth. Good God, don't you, too, Gerry?'

'Naturally,' I said. Then, as a quick thought came to me, I looked at Trent. 'By the way, where were you yesterday morning, Trent?' I asked. 'Here?'

He shook his head and gave me a sneer. 'Nope.'

'Well, where were you?' I pushed him.

He yawned and took a turn making me wait while he fixed a drink for himself. He looked at me over the glass with the same sneer. 'Where was I, Barnes?' he drawled. 'Why, in your dame's apartment. Killing a guy with a knife. So, now, beat it! You weren't asked in. Remember?'

I was ninety-nine percent in favor of making something out of that right then and there. But the remaining one percent was just enough common sense to make me keep my pants on. But before I could say anything, Mather was getting in a scolding nickel's worth.

'Oh, stop being an ass, Harry!' he chided. 'Why shouldn't Gerry ask? He's working on the case. And you, Rita, Beth Price and I were in Paula's apartment after the murder. That's reason enough, so stop it!'

All that from dear, sweet Clyde was no end surprising to me. I thought I even caught the under-note of an order. And surprising, also, was the sullen glare Trent shot him before he wilted out of his nasty pose.

'Okay, skip it, Barnes,' he said to me. 'I was right here. About twelve that Rollins dame phoned for a luncheon date. Sucker I was, I made one, and afterward met her darling once-was! Now git!'

I didn't git. Not to the door. I went to him, yanked him out of the chair and belted him one, but good. Sweet Clyde stifled a scream, but I just stood there watching Trent pinwheel to the floor where he took a nine count before he got slowly to his feet. I waited for him to come for me, but he didn't. He wiped some claret from his nose, and looked like he was going to cry.

'Get out!' he said in a strangled voice. 'Get the hell out of my apartment before I kill you, you damn gumshoe!'

Maybe I would have taken him up on that, too, but Mather was over beside me, his hand on my arm, and the stink of his hair oil in my nose.

'Come, Gerry, I'll go with you,' he said. 'Must run along, really. Harry! Pull yourself together and get some sense, will you? I'll give you a ring later. Come, Gerry, please!'

I don't know just why, but anyway I let Mather lead me out of the apartment while Trent stood there glaring at the two of us. Dear Clyde hung onto my arm all the way to the elevator. When we were inside and on the way down, I shook off his hand.

'You sounded real chummy with Trent,' I said dryly. 'How long have you known him?'

'Oh, a year or more, I'd say,' was his reply. 'Met him at a USO affair. Found out we had several mutual friends. Gerry, I'd like to talk to you.'

We were ground floor by then, so I waited until we were headed for the street. 'Go ahead,' I grunted. 'Talk.'

'Not here,' he said, and held the door for me. 'Do you expect to be in your office this afternoon?'

'I can arrange it, I guess,' I said offhandedly, and suddenly realized he was steering me toward two thousand dollars' worth of maroon and chrome automobile parked at the curb.

'Fine! Say around three, eh? By the by, can I drop you off somewhere?'

Me, I wouldn't be seen dead in that dolled-up heap of his. I shook my head, and let him slide in by himself. 'No thanks,' I said. 'But what do you want to talk to me about?'

He jabbed the starter, and the thing under the hood really did have a sweet purr. He looked up at me and smiled. 'About a Mr. White, Gerry.'

I took that one smack on the chin, but somehow I didn't fall down. I just exploded. '*White?*'

'Why, yes!' As if I should have known all along. 'I've been his attorney for years. I am a lawyer, you know.'

'And you know White?' I mumbled, trying desperately hard to get it all.

'Certainly!' He smiled. 'And, Gerry — though I don't care much for you as a person, I do admire your determination to become a success, without money being the incentive, so I suggested your name to Mr. White.'

'*You what?*' I practically yelled.

'Exactly! To have you help him find the mysterious Mr. A. P. Jordan. 'Bye, Gerry. Three o'clock.'

And with my bare face hanging out, I stood there like a frozen chump while he tooled away from the curb and became lost in traffic.

13

I guess it was all of two minutes I stood there on the curb staring at the traffic that had swallowed up Mather's new car. Then I came out of my trance and mentally kicked myself for the walking dummy I seemed to be becoming. And then I swung around facing the apartment building and debated whether I should try to wangle a passkey and go up to Paula's apartment for I didn't know what, or go back up to Trent's and finish off what I had started. If only to take my mind off other things.

The debate ended in a draw. I mean, I couldn't make up my mind. Then I canceled the whole thing because of another thought. The Club Royale. Maybe Rita had been there, and somebody would know where she had gone. So I flagged a cab and gave him the Royale's address. But it was a waste of cab fare. The two or three members of the hired help I talked to hadn't seen Rita since the night before last. With a knowing smirk, they suggested that I take in the night show and see the lady then. I played the yokel, and left a note with them for Rita to phone me at the office number. And I gave them five bucks to split up, and left. If Rita did show up later, they'd see she got my note, because maybe the star-struck boob would be around again someday with another five!

Twice in a row I wasted cab fare, the second time on a trip down to Centre Street police headquarters to see Bierman. He wasn't in, and nobody seemed to know where he was. But maybe that was because all cops dislike private dicks. Anyway, I learned nothing. So I went out and took a cab to a place that did pay off. To a nice little restaurant I know where it's quiet and nice, and a guy can think. And I was certainly one lad in town who had an awful lot of thinking to do. Thus far, a hundred and one loose ends were sticking out of the whole cockeyed business. If I could only connect up a couple of them, that at least would be something. I didn't, but I did have a swell lunch.

Then I went to the office. A dozen letters had been dropped through the door slot. I breathed a prayer that one was a telegram from Washington, D.C., but I lost. All twelve were sales letters for things I didn't need and never would. I dumped the lot in the waste basket, went to my private liquor cabinet and had a drink. Then I parked at the desk and did some phoning.

First call was to Beth Price's home in Larchmont. She wasn't home, and wasn't expected home until she arrived. I hoped maybe that Paula had made it a short lunch with Mather, but she wasn't at the Biltmore. Three tries at Rita's number got me nothing. And so did maybe five or six other calls. By the time I gave up, it was a little before two o'clock. So I had another drink.

I was contemplating a second one when the breaks swung around my way. The door opened, and in flew Rita. And I mean flew. She kicked the door shut, and stood hands on hips — black eyes burning holes through the air at me.

'You louse! Who the hell do you think you are, doing that?'

The torch of worry I'd been carrying around all morning went out quick. 'You louse, yourself!' I barked. 'Where the hell have you been?'

She looked puzzled, and still angry. She came over to the desk. 'Dammit, Gerry, why did you make a mess of the place? Why, half my things are absolutely ruined? I — I — Darling, I just don't get it!'

'I do, or did!' I growled. 'My head almost caved in. Sit down! We've got talk to make.'

She sat down because I pushed up a chair, and hitched my own right over in front of hers.

'We'll start at the beginning,' I said. 'Why that screwy phone call? What did you want to see me about?'

'I was scared, Gerry,' she said, and looked it even then. 'Scared silly, honest.'

'Why?'

'Early this morning, Gerry — oh,

around six — somebody tried to get into the apartment.'

'Nuts!'

'Nuts, hell!' she blazed. 'I saw them turning the doorknob from the outside. Then they tried a key. I was so terrified I didn't have sense enough to scream. Gerry, I want to get out of there. Find me another place, will you?'

'In New York?' I jeered. 'You and a million other people. You just had a dream, Rita. But what I — '

'Dream, your father's mustache!' she shouted at me. 'Somebody *did* try to get in. I swear it. Twice, too. After the second time, I called you.'

I looked at her and just had to believe. I thought of the mess I'd found in her apartment and looked at her again. 'Why would anybody want to get in?' I asked. 'And tear your place upside down the way he, or they, did?'

'Then you didn't, Gerry? I thought maybe because you were sore, you — '

'My God!' I exploded. 'You've seen me sore enough times. Did I ever wreck your joint?'

'No, no, you didn't,' she said, frowning. 'But it just doesn't make sense. I've nothing but some jewelry and a few personal papers. And — and say, why didn't you wait like I asked in my note?'

'What note?'

'The note I left on the table telling you to wait. It was more than an hour, but you could have waited. I even left the door open so that you could go on in and be sure to see the note.'

I had to take time out to decide if she was crazy, or I was just hearing strange noises.

'Look!' I finally managed, and held up two fingers. 'Twice somebody tries to bust in, so you say. Yet you up and go off leaving the door *open*. You should have *your* head examined!'

She seemed to think so, because as it dawned she gasped and clapped a hand to her ruby lips. 'My God, I didn't even think!' she gulped. 'I — I got a call from the club. Something was supposed to be wrong with the contract. They wanted me over right away. I was so flustered that it was really something serious, I forgot all about anything else. But I did think to leave you that note, Gerry.'

'I didn't get it,' I said, sidestepping the opening she left. 'Was it serious?'

'I don't know. Nobody was in when I got there. I've tried a dozen times to reach Carol Willis, the owner, but no soap each time.'

'Was it Willis who called you?'

'No. He said he was one of the lawyers. But I couldn't get it over the phone. Heintz, or Rice, or something like that. Anyway, I — '

She stopped short as though her windpipe had been cut. Her eyes and mouth opened together. The expression was as dumbfounded as they come. I sighed and nodded.

'You need more sleep,' I said. 'You catch on too damn slow.'

'It's — it's the singing contract,' she stumbled. 'Got me so I don't know whether I'm coming or going. But, my God! So that was a trick to get me out so somebody could go through my apartment? But why, Gerry, why?'

146

'Maybe some guy's wife for spite,' I grunted. And cocking a brow, 'Could be?'

'You can go straight to hell!' she said fiercely, and started to flounce up onto her feet. 'I'm sorry I came!'

I flounced her right back down again. 'Nuts, I was kidding. Where have you been since you returned?'

She played too sore to speak to me for about five seconds. But maybe I do have a way with women like Rita. She melted to a pretty pout. 'Right there, trying to straighten things up,' she said. 'And phoning you every damn place I thought you might be. I finally decided to come here and camp until you showed up. But Gerry, you might at least have picked up a few things. The things you'd given me, anyway.'

If I blushed, I didn't feel it. 'I was too busy picking up myself!' I snapped. 'When I went in somebody clouted me cold. I — '

'Oh, my poor Gerry darling!' And she was in my lap. I pushed her right off, with a slight touch of reluctance. 'A place for everything,' I grunted. 'And right now it's a serious business.'

She made a face at me, crossed her legs, and folded her hands on the billboard-sized purse in her lap.

'Speaking of which,' she said, 'what's new with Paula's troubles? Who was the guy, and who killed him?'

'To both questions, damned if I know,' I admitted. 'But here's one thing I want you to tell me. And straight, too. What was the battle with Trent last night all about?'

Her winning smile faded promptly. She tossed her head and sniffed almost like the way Paula does. 'That ten-cent sailor!' she spat out. 'Just because he'd spent a few dollars on me, he suddenly got the idea he owned me. Nobody owns Rita Rollins!'

The look she gave me said lots of things, but I went into the big brother role quickly. 'Good, keep it like that,' I said. 'So Trent wouldn't take no, and you tossed him out? Could be. I had a couple of words with him this morning. He kind of hates your guts, sister.'

She sniffed twice. 'Mutual!' she snapped.

'Take me to lunch, darling. I'm starved!'

'Can't, got a business date,' I said with a glance at the clock. 'Besides, I'm not through talking. I'm interested in Trent, I — '

'Good God, Gerry!' she broke in. 'You think Harry knifed that fellow's throat in Paula's bedroom?'

I didn't answer for a moment because I was too busy doing a whole lot of hard thinking. But presently I shrugged. 'That remains to be proved,' I said slowly. 'Right now I'm more interested in why. Do you know anything about his war record? The planes he flew, his outfit, and all that sort of stuff?'

Rita went thoughtful, and then nodded. 'A little,' she said, 'though he never talked much about the war. He just wanted to forget it and raise hell. But he was pilot of a torpedo plane. And I think he got a few zeros and a Jap destroyer.'

'What was the number of his torpedo squadron?' I asked.

'I don't know,' she said. 'Anyway, I don't remember that he ever told me. But why the interest?'

'Just curious,' I shrugged it off. Then, casually, 'By the way, did you know that Trent and Clyde Mather have known each other for quite a while?'

I thought she started to nod, but I was wrong. She looked at me, wide-eyed and puzzled. 'Who told you that?' she asked. 'I thought Clyde met Harry the same night I did. At Beth Price's party at the Royale.'

'Oh, it's just something I found out in my travels,' I grunted.

'Made any other progress in your travels, darling?' she asked me after a long pause.

I grinned and looked wise. 'A couple of things,' I said. Then, with a gesture, 'Well, if you come up with any idea who searched your place, let me know fast!'

'I hope to God I do!' she said, tight-lipped. 'He was a stinker, whoever he was, scaring the hell out of me, and making all that mess. So you're throwing me out, darling?'

That last was with a pretty, pretty purr that was most inviting. But I had too many new thoughts to be tempted. 'Right, scram,' I said with a grin. 'Beat it now, and maybe Paula and I will take in your debut under contract tonight. Might even work up a party or something.'

Her eyes clouded, and then went clear almost instantly. 'Just you would be so much better,' she said with a third-act curtain sigh. 'But the Rollins doesn't have to get hit on the head with a brick to catch. Okay, do that. Oh, gosh, wait a minute!'

With that, she started fumbling with her purse clasp and looking around the walls of the office. She finally got the purse open and pulled out a heavy sealed manila envelope. When she put it on the desk, I saw that she'd scrawled her name across the face.

'Since you won't let me bunk in with you, darling, until I get over my jitters, will you do me another favor?'

'This?' I said, and pointed at the envelope.

'Yes, put it in your safe for me, will you?' she asked. 'It isn't much. Some War Bonds, and personal papers, and stuff. I've been keeping it in the apartment, but I'm scared to, now. You'll do it, won't you, Gerry?'

'Sure, if it'll make you feel better.' I shrugged. 'What about your jewelry, though? You — '

'The pieces that are any good I'm going to wear, or hock,' she said. And for the first time I noticed that she was slightly more bejeweled than usual.

'Okay,' I said.

And taking the envelope, I went over to the wall safe, opened it up, and slid the thing in. Then I went back to the desk and wrote out a receipt for one manila envelope, sealed, and contents unknown.

'This makes it legal,' I said, and gave it to her.

She reached for it just as her purse slipped out of her other hand. It hit the floor with a thud: She beat me to picking it up.

'My God, are you carrying the furniture around in that for safekeeping, too?' I laughed.

'No.' She grinned. 'But they do make compacts and stuff so damn heavy these days. Well, darling, kiss me, and I'll go.'

I did, and she went.

14

When Rita hipped her way out of my office, with a final kiss blown back at me, my desk clock registered ten minutes after two. When the hands pointed to four-thirty, I was still sitting at the desk waiting for Clyde Mather to show up. The wait, however, had not been a waste of time. Just in case Bierman, or Bill Hatch, had unearthed something I didn't know about, I sent out for all the latest editions. I read the story carefully in each one. All were simply rehashes of last night's and this morning's papers. In short, an unknown man had been found stabbed to death by Miss Paula Grant in her luxurious East Side apartment. And that the police were working on the case, and an important announcement was expected shortly, blah, blah, blah. Just those bare facts, and nothing more.

I was deep in troubled thought, when

at four-fifteen there came a knock on the door and it was pushed open. No, it wasn't Mather. It was Western Union, and I almost knocked the kid over in my eagerness to grab the yellow envelope out of his hand. But I gave him a buck for his trouble, and he went out with a smile. Me, I ripped open the envelope and pulled out the folded sheet inside. The wire was fairly long, in two parts, and read:

Ex-Lieut. (j.g.) Jordan Parsons Akerson, Pilot, Torpedo Squadron Ten Jan. Forty Four to Oct. Forty Four when dishonorably discharged for theft and sale of Government property. Shot down in Carolines Feb. Forty-four. Turret gunner killed in crash. Tunnel gunner died of injuries. Buried on island of crash by Akerson. Akerson rescued by passing patrol plane May Forty-four. Returned active duty July. War record poor. Bad character. Wanted by navy Intelligence for questioning. Please advise if present address known.

Lieut. (j.g.) Henry Wallace Trent, USNR. Now on terminal leave your city. War record good. Pilot Torpedo Squadron Ten September Forty-four to VJ Day. Any connection between two? Interested.

The wire, of course, was signed, but I'm omitting the name because technically my friend could get himself into hot water for the favor rendered. And the day may come when I may want another favor or two out of him.

Anyway, there it was in black and white. I mean black and yellow. The unknown corpse was no longer unknown. At least to me, but as I remembered Bill Hatch's remark of the morning, I wondered if it was the same with Bierman. Using FBI channels, he might have been able to get this same information in a hurry. But the ego in me hoped plenty that he hadn't.

And while I grinned, dream-picturing the look on Bierman's face when I told him, which I intended to do right after my little talk with Mather, the door opened again. This time there was no knock, because in came Kirby and Jake the Ape. Jake had both hands in sight, but Kirby had only his left hand. The right was in his jacket pocket, just like it had been that morning. I made a savage mental note to throw away my trick shoulder holster and carry my gun in my hand, if I ever intended to get any good out of it. But when I took a second look at Jake I felt a little better. He had a beautiful lump over his right eye, and he walked with a heart-pleasing limp.

'This time we go, Barnes!' Kirby said through his teeth. 'Which way is up to you. Just hold it!'

I am no dope in such a situation. I had both my hands in plain view on the desk when they came in. And so I kept them there while Kirby moved forward and around in back of me, and took away my gun. When he stepped around in front of my desk again he was smiling pleasantly. With his lips only. He casually tossed my gun over his shoulder, and Jake caught it.

'Well?' he said smoothly. 'Ever get

gun-whipped by an expert, Barnes? Jake, here, is an expert. You feel it plenty, but there's hardly a mark to show.'

'No, Kirby,' I said, 'I've never been gun-whipped. But to tell you the truth, there's no need. I want to see White just as much as he wants to see me.'

'Wise boy,' Kirby grunted with a smirk. 'Then we'll get going.'

'Not yet,' I told him pleasantly. 'I'm waiting for somebody. Sit down. You, too, ape.'

Jake made sounds in his throat and took a couple of steps toward me.

'Back, Jake.' Kirby didn't raise his voice, but the steel in it stopped Jake cold as though he'd been kicked in the belly. 'Leave a note for your friend, Barnes,' Kirby said to me.

'He's no friend of mine,' I replied, enjoying it all and inwardly praying that Mather, or somebody, would come through the door. 'Fact is, he's a friend of White's. Works for him, anyway.'

Kirby blinked, and for the first time I saw something besides a cobra's glint in his eyes. I took it for confusion.

'Who works for White?' he wanted to know.

'Clyde Mather,' I said, and deliberately lighted a cigarette. 'He's White's lawyer, they tell me. Met him, haven't you?'

Kirby's expression didn't change, save that his mean eyes narrowed a little.

'Yeah,' he said. 'I've met Mather. When did you last see him?'

'This morning,' I told him. 'And I expect him to drop in any minute now.'

'Maybe he won't,' Kirby said, his damn eyes glued to mine. 'Anyway, we won't wait for him. Let's go.'

'No,' I said.

'Yes,' said Kirby. And, without turning his head, 'Jake!'

But Jake didn't do anything because at that instant my phone bell shrilled. I grabbed it before Kirby could move.

'This is Bierman, Barnes,' said the voice at the other end. 'Come down to my office right away, will you?'

'I'd like to, Lieutenant Bierman,' I said, and looked at Kirby. 'But a couple of clients seem to want to use force. Perhaps you know them. One's name is — '

I stopped for a chuckle, because I never saw two people go out of my sight so fast. The door slam sounded like a pistol shot. At least to Bierman at the other end of the line.

'What was that a shot?' he barked.

'No, just my clients leaving,' I told him. 'I'll be down right away. But what — '

'It can wait until you get here,' he cut me off. 'But hurry it up!'

I did, but with certain precautions. I mean, I took the elevator to the second floor, and walked the rest of the way down the rear fire exit stairs, and on out to the street that paralleled the one in front. Luck sent a cab cruising by at that moment, and it took me the rest of the way down to Centre Street police headquarters. When I walked into Bierman's office it was to find that he was not alone. And for the second time in as many days I was half-pleased and half-displeased to see Bill Hatch's grinning face. And when from behind Bierman's back he flashed me some kind of a high sign, I was also puzzled. And a trifle worried, too, because the air in the place seemed charged with a high-voltage current. Bierman, though, was still smooth. His smile was cordial enough, and so was his gesture at a nearby chair.

'Thanks for making it fast, Barnes,' he said, and held out a silver case. 'Cigarette?'

I took one, and a light from him, too. Through smoke I glanced at Hatch, but he wasn't looking at me now. He was fiddling with a shade cord and staring out the window. I frowned, leaned back, and looked at Bierman.

'So?' I said with a grin. 'What's it now?'

'How are you coming along, Barnes?' Bierman asked.

'A little,' I told him. 'And you?'

'A little, too,' he said, and plucked a flake of tobacco off his lower lip. 'I asked you down here, Barnes, for a little help . . . if you don't mind?'

I did mind the soothing smile, and the arched eyebrow, but I let it slide.

'No, I don't mind,' I said. 'Anyway, not yet. What kind of help?'

'Good,' he said. Then snubbing out his butt, he leaned his arms on the desk and laced his fingers. 'The four people who dropped into Miss Grant's apartment, before you called me,' he said quietly, 'what do you know about them?'

'A lot,' I replied instantly. Then, with a glance toward the window, 'But so does Hatch.'

Bill turned his head for an instant and gave me a look that was supposed to tell me something. But I didn't get it at all. Nor did I bother over it for long. I looked back at Bierman.

'I'll change that to three of them,' I said. 'I only met Trent for the first time yesterday.'

I guess I must have let something slip into my voice, because the sudden ghost of a smile whipped across Bierman's lips.

'You don't like Trent, do you?' he asked.

'No, I don't,' I told him frankly. Then, adding quickly, 'But that doesn't mean he isn't okay to others.'

Bierman half-nodded as though to tell me he got what I meant. And then he practically fired the next question at me.

'And you don't like Mather, either, do you?'

I suddenly thought that Bill Hatch had been working his mouth, and the glare I flung at the back of his head was impulsive.

'I don't like or dislike Mather,' I told Bierman. 'To me he's just a wet smack trying to act the playboy. He — What the hell is this all about, anyway?'

A little bird was egging me into anger, and the eye I gave Bierman was well-frosted. But he didn't scare at all.

'If he's no more than that to you, why did you threaten him this morning because he was taking Miss Grant to lunch?'

Maybe that sixth sense they call premonition had steeled me. I don't know. Anyway, I didn't go straight up out of my chair as I normally would. Instead, I sat stone-still and stared hard at Bierman to catch the first sign of a gag. And he just sat there and looked back at me.

'Who threatened who, where, and when?' I finally got out. 'And who says so?'

'Trent,' Bierman replied. 'In his apartment this morning.'

'Nuts!' I said as I went a little out of control. 'So that heel told you I threatened Mather?'

Bierman just nodded, and watched my face. I blew up. 'Trent is a damn liar! Why, I left his place with Mather, and made a date with him to meet in my office at three. Of all the lousy — '

I stopped short, because about then the curtain parted in the brain, and the clear white light began to shine through. I swallowed hard, and leaned way out of my chair, my eyes fixed on Bierman. A screwy kind of roaring was filling my ears.

'For God's sake, Bierman, do you mean that Clyde Mather . . . ?'

I didn't get a chance to finish the question. The door opened at that instant, and in came Sergeant Goff. He didn't even glance my way. He went over to Bierman and placed an envelope on his desk.

'Here it is, and the report, sir,' he said.

'Thanks,' Bierman said, and made a

faint motion with his hand for Goff to leave.

Goff did, and Bierman leaned back in his chair, opened the envelope and took out a sheet of paper. He read it, refolded it and placed it on his desk. Then he spread the envelope opening, peered inside, and finally looked across the desk at me.

'Have you your gun on you?' he asked.

I felt the red leap to my face, and tried desperately to check it. I shook my head. 'No,' I said, and pulled back my jacket to show him the empty holster. Then, as the pot boiled over, 'Dammit, Bierman, what in all hell is this about?'

For an answer, Bierman lifted the envelope, open side down. A small hunk of something dropped out and hit the desk blotter with a thud. One look and I saw that it was a fired bullet of small caliber. I looked at Bierman, and didn't even bother counting ten.

'Cut the act!' I clipped at him. 'You're simply building up to nothing, because I don't know a damn thing. Who's been shot? Clyde Mather?'

'Why do you name Mather?' he pumped at me.

My respect for Bierman's technique was sliding downhill, but fast.

'It's obvious!' I told him. 'Your merry-go-round talk. Are you going to tell me, or do we play a guessing game?'

The mildness went out of his eyes for the first time. They flashed a little, and his jaw squared. 'Don't get tough, Barnes!' he said. 'It'll get you nowhere. Yes, it was Mather. He was found shot in his apartment a little before three this afternoon.'

'By Trent,' I said flatly. 'And Trent called you.'

It was a couple of wild guesses, but they zinged straight home. Bierman shot me a surprised look. 'How did you know?' he rapped out.

'I didn't!' I shot back at him. 'I guessed. Because of his lies to you about me threatening Mather. And the reason he put the spikes to me, Bierman, is because he used some foul words about a friend of mine, and I knocked them down his throat. And if you'll have Trent sent in

165

here I'll beat the truth out of him so that you can hear it!'

Small time guff? Sure it was, but I was burning up so fast I wasn't doing any thinking before opening the yap. However, it did have its effect on Bierman. He gave a quick little shake of his head, and half lifted one hand in a gesture.

'Keep your shirt on, Barnes,' he told me. 'I didn't say I believed Trent.'

'Well, you sure acted it,' I said, like a kid.

Bierman sighed like an exasperated parent, and that didn't help me to cool off either. He spent a couple of minutes studying some notes on his desk, and then looked at me again.

'Mather was killed sometime between two-thirty and quarter to three,' he said, as though he were reading notes aloud. 'At five minutes to three Trent called at his apartment. The door was partly opened, the bottom had caught on a scatter rug, so he went in and found the body. He called us at three o'clock. The call was put through to me in this office.' Bierman paused for a moment as he picked up the bullet. 'This is the bullet,' he said. 'Through the heart from close range. Ballistics says it's a twenty-five-caliber Luger bullet. There were no signs of struggle in the apartment. Just Mather stretched out on the living room floor. But, of course, we haven't finished with the place yet.'

I heard all of what Bierman said. And then again, I only clearly heard part of it. At the mention of the type and caliber of the murder weapon, the back of my neck started to tingle. And lumps of lead that had been my lunch began to churn around in my stomach. I had a twenty-five Luger at my place. It was one of a pair I had taken from a Japanese major I killed in China a couple of years ago. He was wearing them holster-style, one on either side, à la General Patton, when he walked into my gun sights. I suppose anything heavier would have buckled him at the knees, he was such a shrimp. Anyway, I had taken both guns for souvenirs, and had brought them back to the States.

One of them I had given to Paula for a

gag, telling her she'd probably need it when all the wolves got out of the service, living alone as she was in a wicked, sinful city!

15

'What's the matter, Barnes? You don't look well.'

Bierman's voice snapped me out of my trance, and I hastily changed the expression on my face. Whatever it had been. 'I was thinking,' I said slowly. 'Two murders in two days. Are you connecting them?'

'I'm not connecting anything yet!' he said with a startling show of impatience. 'Tell me, have you seen Miss Grant since her luncheon date with Mather?'

'No,' I said. And then I got mad all over again. 'And for God's sake, don't start that line! Paula was fond of Mather. She would no more shoot him than — '

'Paula's missing, Gerry.'

That was from Bill Hatch by the window. Bierman swung around sharply to snarl, but changed his mind and quickly snapped his eyes back to me. But I beat him to the punch.

169

'I don't even know if she *had* lunch with him!' I said. 'But what do you mean, missing?'

'She isn't at the Biltmore or at her apartment,' Bierman told me.

For reasons I couldn't explain at the moment, I breathed easier. 'So what?' I grunted. 'Paula is an incurable window shopper. You'll probably find her over on Fifth, or Madison, right now. But what about Trent?'

'I've talked with Trent.'

'And let him go?' I couldn't stop from saying. Then, when he nodded, 'Well, I'll find Miss Grant. Then you can talk to her, and let her go, too!'

Bierman didn't like that, and I didn't care a damn.

'Don't tell me my job, Barnes!' he snapped. 'If I want to, I can hold Miss Grant, Trent, *and* you, for twenty-four hours.'

'And why don't you want to, Lieutenant?' I asked sweetly.

He gave me a disgusted look, but let it slide. Instead, he seemed thoughtful and plenty perplexed. 'Because I don't want to yet,' he said, as though talking to himself. 'There's more than just two killings. What's at back of them is — '

'Then you *do* connect them?' I cut in on him.

He looked sore that he'd blabbed, but he nodded. 'For the present,' he said. 'But by the way, what did you mean over the phone . . . a couple of clients seem to want to use force?'

'Oh, that was just a gag,' I said with a quick chuckle. 'A couple of friends were — '

'*What* friends?'

Bierman could make me sore quicker than any man I'd ever met. 'Two guys I was in service with!' I snapped. 'They happened to drop up to rib me, and . . . Look, do you want to know what I had for lunch, too?'

Bierman slapped his hand on the desk and stood up. 'Okay, Barnes, thanks for dropping in,' he said. Then, with disgust dropping from his lips in chunks, 'You private detectives are all alike. Get out of here, and take Hatch with you!'

'A pleasure!' I shot back, and crooked a

finger at Hatch. 'Come, scribbler! We've been asked to leave.'

Hatch turned from the window and gave us both a disgusted look. 'You two talk like a Hollywood script!' he growled, and moved toward the door.

I moved after him, when Bierman stopped me. 'By the way, Barnes, we've identified the corpse.'

'Good,' I said, and grinned. 'So've I.'

He didn't like that much, but he tried hard not to show it. 'That tattooing was not his initials,' he said.

'You thought that, I didn't.' And I grinned some more. 'I knew that it was his navy squadron identification. A lot of the fellows had themselves marked that way. His stood for Torpedo Bomber Squadron Number Ten. They flew Grumman Avengers, in case you didn't find that out, too.'

'Thanks,' he said dryly.

'Not at all.' I walked out after Hatch, softly closing the door behind me.

When we were down on the sidewalk, hunting for a cruising cab, Bill looked at me with scorn, and spoke with twice as much. 'You *should* be in the movies! What ham! What a dope! Just plain corn!'

'Which is just one man's opinion.' I grinned at him, and then whistled at a cab coming along. It was taken and went rolling on by.

'You make me sick!' Bill exploded. 'What the hell did it get you? Look, Frank Bierman knows his stuff, or he wouldn't be holding down that job. Now, just a little cooperation from you and — '

'In your hat!' I snapped him off. 'Anybody who thinks I go around killing people, I just don't like. A trait of the Barnes family for centuries back.'

'Kid's stuff!' Hatch growled. 'Bierman doesn't suspect you. And I don't think he suspects Paula, either. He's just fishing around for something.'

'Such as?' I asked him.

Bill Hatch sighed and shook his head. 'When I can fathom Bierman's methods I'll write a book about it,' he said. 'Do you think Trent shot Clyde? And if so, why?'

'To quote your Homicide, pal,' I countered, 'I'm not thinking anything yet.

But here's another reason Bierman gets my cork. What the hell business did he have telling Mather that Paula was at the Biltmore?'

'Says who?' Hatch demanded quickly.

'Mather,' I told him. 'He said so this morning.'

'Mather is a liar,' Bill snapped. 'Or was a liar. He did call Bierman but Frank told him to go chase. I was in Bierman's office when the call came through.'

'Then who did tell Mather?' I asked myself aloud.

Hatch didn't seem to hear. He was off on something else.

'So you know who the dead guy was, huh?' he said. 'Your dumb play to Bierman was obvious. You know, you're disappointing me, pal. I was cheering so loud for you.'

I didn't bother with the crack that came to mind. Frankly, it was just so much chitchat, and I wanted to get rid of Bill and go on the hunt for Paula, and find her before Bierman or one of his men did. And my plans were helped along splendidly because at that moment an empty cab hove into sight. I flagged it and the driver saw me.

'Where can I drop you off, hitchhiker?' I asked Bill as we piled in.

'No you don't!' he said firmly. 'I think I'll tag along for a while. Might be interesting to see how the other half works.'

'Okay,' I said, smiling. 'You can lay out some clean clothes for me while I'm taking a shower.'

And leaning forward, I gave the cabby my apartment address. Hatch rode in silence, a set, stubborn look on his face, as far as the mid-town section. There he seemed to make up his mind about something.

'Pull in at the next corner!' he called to the cabby. Then, giving me a nasty look, 'In your lousy mood you probably wouldn't offer me a drink. So the hell with you. But good luck, chum.'

'Same to you, pal.' I grinned as he got out.

He turned long enough to salute with thumb to nose, and then walked away. I took the cab seven blocks more toward my apartment, and then told the driver to cut over and down to the Biltmore. I didn't have any plan of action, except to first find out if Paula had checked out of the hotel.

Well, I found out at the desk that she hadn't, but wasn't in her room. And as I turned to head for the outside phone booths, I bumped into Nick on his way to the cashier's nook to get somebody's check cashed. He stopped and gave a backward jerk of his head.

'In the corner at my station, Mr. Barnes,' he said. 'Been waiting half an hour. And if you'll excuse me, I think she's upset about something.'

'Thanks, Nick,' I said, and relief started in at my toes and flooded all the way up. 'Bring me the usual when you get a chance.'

'Two minutes,' Nick assured me.

I went into the cocktail lounge at the clock end, and looked to my right. There she was making rings on the table with her glass, and looking beautiful, tired, and slightly annoyed. She was so busy thinking about something that she didn't see me until I'd slid into a chair. Her smile was any way I wanted to take it.

'Well, well, the chief, no less! What'll you have, Chief?'

What I had was the sudden thought that Paula had had a couple too many. And the shine in her eyes seemed to bear that out.

'I saw Nick on the way in,' I said. 'And just where the hell have you been?'

'Here, there, and about, darling. Why?'

'Nothing, no reason,' I said, and watched her. 'Only, the cops happen to be looking for you.'

She seemed to flinch for an instant, and then her laugh was about half a tone too high. 'Cops!' she said, and wrinkled her nose. 'When we're married, my pet, can't we live where there are no cops? But I suppose the poor guy has a right to be sore at me.'

'Who, and why?' It was my turn to want to know.

'Bierman's shadow,' she said, and giggled. 'He practically rode on the running board of my taxi. But Clyde saved the day. Clyde's really clever, Gerry. I bet that shadow's still looking for me up in the Bronx.'

'Where did you have lunch?' I asked, and tried to keep the edge out of my voice.

'The Colony. And it was delicious. Clyde can suggest the nicest things. You should learn more about good foods, darling.'

'When did you finish lunch?' I asked.

'One-thirty, I guess.' Then, with a sharp look at me, 'What is this, the jealous husband routine?'

I didn't reply. Nick arrived with my drink, guessed that we were throwing high hard ones at each other, and left us with a smile.

'Then you left Mather at one-thirty, huh?' I said when I'd sampled my drink.

'No, though it's none of your business,' Paula said. 'From the Colony we went to his apartment. He wanted to pick up some papers.'

'And then?' I prodded.

She giggled at me over her drink. 'Mr. Barnes, *really*!'

'Nuts!' I snapped. 'Cut it, Paula. I want to know what time you left Mather. Dammit, tell me!'

I should have left out the last. She got really sore. The drinks in her helped, too.

'Do you? Well, it's none of your damn business! Until you lead me down the aisle, boyfriend, I'll do as I — '

Her voice was going up the scale, so I cut her off. 'Shut up!' I said. 'I want to know because Mather was shot a little after half past two. Now will you stop clowning?'

If Paula was a little high, she suddenly wasn't anymore. Her face paled, and the crazy shine went out of her eyes like a snuffed light. She reached over and clutched my hand. 'Gerry, no! You're kidding! Clyde Mather was . . . was . . . ?'

She stumbled, and I saw real tears come into her eyes. I guess she had been sort of fond of the guy, and for a moment or two I felt a little cheap.

'It's true, sweet,' I said gently. 'He was shot in his apartment. The gun was a twenty-five-caliber Luger.'

I watched her closely as I spoke the

last, but it didn't seem to register at all.

'Who shot him?' she asked. Then, a little wild, 'But Gerry, who would shoot a kind, thoughtful, and inoffensive person like Clyde?'

'That's not known yet,' I told her. 'Trent found him. And he told Bierman you had a luncheon date with Mather. What time *did* you leave him?'

'A little before two,' she said, brows puckered. 'Yes, because I remember looking at my watch when he let me out in front of Lord and Taylor's. Oh, Gerry, I feel perfectly awful. Poor Clyde. He . . . Signal Nick and order me another drink, will you?'

'Yeah, but I want a smoke first,' I said.

And as I said it, I nonchalantly picked up her purse on the table, unsnapped it, and started rummaging, as though for a pack of cigarettes. I suddenly felt Paula's eyes burning holes through the side of my head. And I saw her push a pack of Luckies across the table. When I glanced up, I saw a sudden flash of loathing in her eyes that made me gulp. Without saying a word, she reopened the purse, took out a bunch of keys, and tossed them down in front of me.

'*My* twenty-five-caliber Luger is in my lower bureau drawer, where I put it the day you gave it to me!' she said, tight-lipped. Then, as her lower lip trembled, 'Oh, Gerry, you louse, you heel, you stinker . . . how could you!'

I wanted to speak, to say anything, but I just couldn't get the tongue to move. All the emotions possible in such a situation flooded through me like liquid flame. I wanted nothing out of life but to take Paula in my arms, beg her forgiveness, and then step off the top of a tall building.

I did manage to open my mouth to start begging, but not a sound came out. That, however, was because at that exact moment I saw Kirby get up from a table way over on the other side, bow to somebody, and put on his hat and walk out. And by half-rising and craning my neck I was able to see who he had bowed to.

It was Beth Price!

16

'Don't go, Gerry! But you really were a louse. That was definitely despicable. Besides, why would I shoot Clyde? Or anybody?'

I sank back into my chair, half my thoughts on Paula, and the other half on what I'd just seen. I made my expression shamefaced and contrite.

'I'm worse than that, and I'm sorry as hell, darling,' I said. 'I must be nuts. But this thing is slowly driving me crazy. I'm almost beginning to suspect myself. Can you forgive me, huh?'

She smiled, but not with the usual warmth quota. 'Skip it,' she said. 'But is it as bad as that? Haven't you found out anything?'

I touched a finger to my eye and groaned. 'About as much as you could put in here,' I said. 'But I have hopes. I mean, at least I've got a couple of ideas that may eventually turn into something.'

Paula leaned forward, all eager attention. 'What ideas, Gerry?' she asked.

'Well — ' I began. And that's as far as I got.

'Paula, dearest! And you, Gerry! Oh, Paula, I've tried dozens of times to get you on the phone. Where have you been? Don't tell me the silly police arrested you?'

It was Beth Price, looming over our table and gushing.

'Hello, Beth,' Paula said as I got up. 'Sit down with us, darling. No, I'm still a free woman. My, but you look scrumptious!'

'You like it?' Beth gurgled and flounced down into the chair I'd toe-hooked over. 'Daddy will kill me when he gets the bill. But I don't care. Oh, I shouldn't have said that, should I? I'm sorry, darling.'

'What'll you have, Beth?' I said, and caught Nick's eye. 'And who was your boyfriend?'

'Oh, any old thing, sweet,' she gushed. Then, with the well-known kitten look, 'Isn't he cute? That's Ted Kirby. I met him at the Club Royale a couple of nights ago. You should meet him, Paula. He has

183

such fascinating eyes. But now, tell me all about it. I'm just dying to hear. It must have been terrible, wasn't it?'

'Yes,' Paula said, and her voice was flat. 'So let's not talk about it, shall we? I'm trying to forget.'

I thought Beth was going to crawl over into her lap, she was so sorry. 'Of course we won't, darling!' she burst forth, and patted one of Paula's hands. 'I say the damnedest things, don't I? But things like that intrigue me so!'

'You and several others in New York,' I said to myself. And then I gave Nick the orders, and steered the conversation into the routine chitchat channels. Five minutes later, though, we were all down at the bottom of the word well. And so Beth threw another pitch. At me this time.

'But you're going to solve it and become famous, aren't you, Gerry?' she purred.

'I'll settle for just solving it.' I grinned. And then, because it didn't seem I had anything to lose, I said, 'And maybe you can help me out.'

'Me?' she trilled. And you would have thought I was holding out a mink coat. 'Oh, how thrilling! I'd just love to help solve a murder mystery. What do I do, Gerry? Tell me, quick!'

'Think, and answer me a question,' I said, and ignored the lightning that started to flash in Paula's eyes.

'All right, I'm thinking,' the screwy bunny said. 'What's the question?'

Paula kicked, but I had moved both my shins out of range. 'A year or so ago Paula let you use her apartment for a while,' I said. 'Did you ever give the key back to her?'

A funny expression came into the Price kid's eyes, and I got set to duck fast. But I guess it was the beginning of her thinking-hard look, because her brows came together and she tapped the point of her chin with a fingernail that was four shades brighter red than I ever saw on any other woman's finger.

'Now, let me see, what did I do with that key?' she said. Then, wiping of the thoughtful look and beaming at Paula, 'And you were a darling to let me have the apartment, dear. I don't know what I would have done. But let me see. I suppose I didn't give it back to you, did I?'

Before Paula could open her mouth, I flashed her a look that had all the sincere pleading in it that I could drum up.

'You probably did, Beth,' she said. 'But I just can't seem to remember. I . . . ' She stopped, and her eyes and mine flew to Beth's face. The Price kid had gasped and clapped her two hands together.

'I remember now!' she cried. 'Oh, Paula, I know you will think me just horrible. But Clyde was so hopelessly in love with you. And he looked so forlorn and miserable, I . . . Well, I just felt so sorry for him. And I thought it would be all right.'

My chair had suddenly become wired, and my spine was getting the full voltage strength. 'What was all right?' I snapped. 'What are you talking about?'

'Why, Gerry Barnes, you old jealous guy! As if anybody meant a thing to Paula, after she met you!'

'Okay, okay, we're mates for life!' I said

with an angry gesture. 'But what about Mather?'

And then she got annoyed. 'Who the hell are you yelling at?' she demanded. 'I've a good mind not to tell you!'

To keep my hands from her throat, I picked up my drink and had some of it. And Paula stepped into the breach.

'Don't mind Gerry, Beth,' she said with a chuckle. 'He's always like this when he has a bellyache. Tell me, dear.'

The Price brat flung me a surly pout, and switched to a beam for Paula. 'Well, it really wasn't anything,' she said. 'And we both know that Clyde is always the perfect gentleman. Anyway, you were due back from wherever you went that time.'

'Chicago, to visit my mother,' Paula said.

'Yes, Chicago, to see your mother.' Beth Price nodded. 'And Clyde wanted to fix up your apartment with some flowers. I was too busy to help him. I was going out of town, myself, that day. Remember you'd been back a whole week before I saw you?'

'Yes, I remember,' Paula murmured.

Then, as sad tenderness stole into her eyes, she said in a low voice, 'So it was Clyde who put all those beautiful flowers in the apartment? I never did find out. Poor dear . . . '

Paula caught herself, and I quickly picked it up from there. 'You mean you gave Clyde the key to Paula's place, Beth?' I said. 'And he didn't give it back?'

'That's right.' She nodded. 'I guess I just clean forgot about it until now. Or I probably figured he'd given it to Paula when he saw her.'

I looked at Paula, and I guess she was waiting for the look.

She shook her head. 'No,' she said in a quiet voice. 'That I would have remembered.'

Beth Price waited out the heavy silence for about fourteen seconds. 'What's the matter, Paula?' she demanded. 'Was that so terribly wrong of me? But, darling, I was simply so sorry! If you could have seen how miserable, how — '

'It was quite okay, Beth,' I broke in on her. Then, when I had her eyes, I said,

'Clyde Mather was shot and killed this afternoon.'

The conglomeration of expressions that shot across her face, and through her eyes, was too fast for me to follow. All I was sure of was the way she clutched her drink to keep from dropping it.

'Good God!' she got out in a weak, strangled voice. 'Do you mean that Clyde Mather was shot in Paula's apartment, too?'

I shook my head, and then I suddenly saw Rita Rollins in back of Paula's chair.

'Who's been shot, chums? Or should I say half-shot, like I think I am? Hi, Paula, Beth, and darling!'

Rita wasn't just half-shot. She was all seas over, or I've never seen a woman under the influence of the firewater. Her eyes were brighter than twinkling stars, yet there was a sort of dull, befuddled stare underneath when I took a second look. I had seen that same thing in a hop-head's eyes, and I was more than a little jolted. I'll say this, though: Rita showed it only in her face, and in the high key of her voice. The rest of her was riding just as steady as the *Queen Mary* in a millpond.

I got up, thumbed her toward my chair, and borrowed another empty one from a nearby table. When I came back, I gave her a crooked grin. 'You taking it in the arm these days?' I asked.

She shot me a looked that should have dropped me dead. 'Go to hell, lover! But first order me a drink. Now, what's all this about somebody getting shot? Who?'

Nick was at my elbow then, so I ordered for Rita the same as the three of us were having. And gave him the sign that meant ninety-nine and nine-tenths parts fizz water. Nick winked to let me know he had caught the signal. I turned back to the table just in time to see Rita take a long pull from my glass. She hitched away when I reached for it.

'No, baby needs this quick,' she said, and finished the darn thing.

All this time, Paula and Beth Price were smiling politely, but not saying a word. Rita looked at them, then at me, and smirked.

'Haven't you nice people ever seen a

drunken lady before?' she demanded. 'Well, take a good look, because I am drunk and I'm going to get drunker. Where the hell is Nick? Out growing the hops?'

'Relax, and cut it out, kid!' I said in a low voice. 'What's biting you, anyway?'

She reached over and patted my cheek. 'For you, darling, anything,' she said. 'I don't know. I just feel lousy. Oh, I'm sorry, everybody.'

The smile that went with it told us that she meant it. Paula and Beth blinked the frost from their eyes. 'Forget it, Rita,' Paula said. 'Us women, you know. And I'll have one with you. Where is Nick, anyway?'

I was just about to open my mouth and tell her that Nick had left his jet-propelled job at home, when I caught on. Paula was one swell gal, and Rita thought so, too.

'You're one swell person, Paula,' she said, and her voice was a little choked. 'And this heel, here, is the luckiest heel I ever met!'

'Thanks,' I growled. 'I really don't deserve it.'

'No, you don't, Gerry.'

That came from Beth Price. And so I was just the lucky sucker who was being allowed to stay and pick up the check. I quickly thought up a sweet retort, but I didn't have a chance to use it. Rita suddenly became conscious of the four thousand odd dollars' worth of clothes Beth was wearing, and a three-way conversation instantly developed in that department. I didn't mind much, though. It gave me a chance to study Rita a little. Oddly enough, she seemed to be sobering up fast, at least in her speech and her actions. But that crazy light did remain in her eyes, and I became more and more certain that Rita was really on edge about something. So certain was I that I leaped at the first lull in the conversation.

'You going to sing tonight, Rita?'

She spun toward me almost tigerishly. 'Why?' It came like a pistol shot.

'Hey, this is me, remember?' I said with a laugh. 'And don't you remember I said Paula and I might drop in for your debut? What time, was all I meant. I don't want to sit around in that crummy joint for hours.'

'Why, Gerry, the Club Royale is tops!' Beth Price protested.

'Like hell it is!' Rita spat out. 'It *is* crummy. And I'm not singing there tonight, or any other night!'

'Why, Rita!' Paula gasped. 'Only yesterday you told us — '

'That was yesterday!' Rita cut her off. 'The contract was just a come-on. Mr. Louse Carol Willis has fired me.'

'You're kidding,' I couldn't help but say. 'Why the hell?'

Rita looked up at me and laughed kind of funny. 'And the king of the wolves wants to know why?' she echoed, sweet-nasty-like.

Nick's arrival with her watered drink stopped me from forgetting I was a heel. She practically snatched it out of Nick's hand, and took a long pull. When she lowered the glass, she lowered it all the way to the table, and then stood up.

'My God, the pals a woman has in this town!' she exploded in seething disgust. 'Give the rest to your damn potted plants,

Nick. And good-bye, my dear friends!'

I caught up with her out in the lobby. 'Rita, for Pete's sake, what gives?' I said sternly. 'The drink was my dumb idea, and I'm sorry. Come on, baby, what's wrong, anyway?'

She looked up at me, and her eyes were like she was crying quietly in her heart. Then the sharp twitch of her lips took it all away.

'Not a thing. Gerry. Not a damn thing. Go on back to them. I'm the fifth wheel. But don't worry. Little Rita knows exactly what to do for little Rita.'

'And just what the hell does that mean?' I demanded, and tightened my grip on her arm.

She jerked her arm and I let it go because it wouldn't have looked nice for us to start wrestling there in the lobby.

'You, my dumb darling, are not the only thing wearing pants in this town,' she said slowly. 'Nor with a nice bank balance, either. Pip-pip, sweet. And thanks for the glass of fizz water!'

I watched her trip lightly down the wide stairs toward the Forty-third Street door. Three marines coming up the stairs stopped long enough to give her the approving eye. Then I went back into the lounge, but only Beth was at the table.

'Paula was wanted on the phone,' she told me before I could ask. 'But, Gerry, what in the world is the matter with Rita? I've never seen her so nasty in all the years I've known her. You know what I think, Gerry?'

'Losing her singing contract, you mean?' I grunted disinterestedly.

'Oh, no, I don't mean that,' she assured me. 'I think the best thing in the world for Rita would be for her to meet and marry some nice rich man.'

That super-brilliant deduction rendered me speechless. And before the Price brat could toss more pearls of wisdom into my lap, Paula came back. 'Well, pals,' she said in a voice that brought me up straight, 'I'll send you a postcard with my address and cell number. And Martha Washington candy is my favorite.'

'Paula, what on earth, darling?' Beth Price gurgled.

'Lieutenant Bierman,' Paula said, but looked at me, 'my presence is requested at police headquarters.'

'I'll go with you,' I said, and reached for my wallet.

'Yes!' Beth exclaimed. 'We'll both go. But why in the world does — '

A gesture from Paula stopped her. 'No, children, you two amuse yourselves,' we were told. Then, in mock tones, 'I must face this alone. Besides, I think the lieutenant is rather fascinating.'

'Nuts!' It slipped out of my mouth. 'Has he got the wagon out front?'

Paula re-tucked her purse under her arm, and made a pass at the thing on her head that was a hat.

'How about dinner around sevenish?' she said. 'We might as well meet here.'

'Love to, darling, but I've a date,' the Price brat said. 'But you're sure, Paula that — '

'Perfectly,' Paula soothed her. Then, with an imp look at me, 'Besides, there are a few questions I want to ask the lieutenant.'

'Then I'll trail along,' I said firmly. 'You

may think Bierman's a lady's man, but don't — '

'Of course I won't, sweet!' Paula chirped brightly. 'Then seven it is, darling, right here with you. 'Bye.'

And away she went, the cynosure of more than one guy's eyes in the place. And about five minutes later Beth Price blew away, too. I thoughtfully paid the check, passed a word or two of chitchat with Nick and Angelo, and then went out to the lobby phone booths and called Carol Willis at the Club Royale.

17

After I'd talked with Willis on the phone, I went into the men's bar and had a drink, and cursed myself for not insisting that I go with Paula to see Bierman. But I knew perfectly well that it wouldn't have gotten me anything. I mean, when Paula makes up her mind on something, even the marines can't change it. So I had another drink as a chaser to the first, and by then I had made up my own mind on a thing or two.

In storybooks, the brilliant detective usually finds a lock of hair, an old calling card, and maybe a wad of gum stuck under a movie house seat. He adds them all up and everything comes out even so that justice can triumph in the end. But as far as I was concerned, all I had come up with was a bunch of hunches, and a couple of half-baked theories. True they added up to come out even, but it was the zero kind of even.

So what to do next? Take all my troubles and worries to Bierman, and watch him go to work? Or should I toss technique and caution over the side, and start swinging from the floor? Maybe it was the scotch in me, but the latter suddenly was appealing. After all, you can't shoot a guy for trying, even though you can slap him behind bars.

Anyway, I decided on quick action, even if I had to create that action myself And instantly I knew just the ideal spot for same. In short, Harry Trent's apartment. So I paid for my drinks and took a cab uptown, paying it off a block from the place. Popping into a drugstore, I called Trent's apartment. He answered, and I disguised my voice and asked for Mr. Smith. He snapped that I had the wrong number and hung up. So did I. So far so good. Trent was in his apartment, which was what I had hoped for. But was he alone?

That was the important question, and one that I could not answer. I might find out by asking in the building lobby, but I didn't want to do that. I mean, I might be recognized, which wouldn't help at all later on. If I was going to gain anything, I just had to come and go unobserved.

It was a chance I had to take, and I took it. Not smart, and maybe just plain stupid. But right then I was all for it, and let the chips fall where they would! I went up in the self-operated private elevator to Paula's floor, and then down the fire exit stairs to Trent's floor. The fact that it was to the left of the elevator near the end was all in my favor. I mean that anybody sticking his head out would naturally look to the right toward the elevators, and not to the left toward the end of the hall.

I came to a halt in front of the apartment door, took a couple of deep breaths, crossed my fingers, said a little prayer to Lady Luck, jabbed the bell button and stepped quickly to my right, and flattened myself back to the wall. I heard Trent's muffled cough, then the clicking of the inside latch. By then my right hand was over my head, fingers extended stiff and straight. The door opened, and I heard his grunt when he didn't see anybody. Then out came his head, and turned as he looked along the hall toward the elevators.

And at that exact instant, down came the edge of my hand on the back of his neck. The old rabbit punch, so to speak, but the force with which I hit the back of Trent's neck was a darn sight more than any rabbit's effort!

Trent keeled over like a water-soaked log, and I caught him before he hit the floor. For a couple of seconds, I just held him in my arms as cold and hot sweat poured from every pore. And then I played it all or nothing, and lugged him back into his own apartment. I won. Lady Luck had answered my prayer. Trent was alone.

Easing him down to the floor, I went to work fast. First I closed and locked the door. Then I took a good look at Trent just to see if he needed more of the same to stay that way. He didn't, but to be on the safe side I tied his arms behind his back with his own belt, and a handkerchief over his eyes so he couldn't peek if he did come to sooner than I expected. And then I set to work on the real part of the mission.

In short, I began searching Trent's apartment. Right off the bat, I found one thing I was looking for: the gun in his service bag in a closet. But it was a disappointment. It was a navy Colt, not a twenty-five-caliber Luger. I tossed it back in with a grunt of disgust, and went on hunting. Five, ten, fifteen minutes flashed by. I hadn't found a thing that would do me any good, let alone tell me anything, and the sweat was beginning to ooze again. A faint groan from Trent on the floor speeded up the flow. And speeded me up, too!

Desk drawers, bureau drawers, two closets, everything where anybody kept things got my eagle-eyed inspection. And all no soap. Not so much as a bobby pin, or a little book of phone numbers to get my attention. Yes, I even bent over Trent and went through his pockets. The amount of money I found in his wallet made me lift an eye, but that's all that its contents did.

'Scram, bright boy! Scram, and fast!'

Maybe I muttered the words aloud, or

maybe I just echoed them in my brain. Anyway, I was convinced that it was the only thing to do. But for a few seconds more, I stood by the living room desk, casting my eyes about in desperate hope of spotting something I had missed, and absently twisting and bending a folded newspaper I had pulled out of the top desk drawer. When I saw nothing else to search, I half-lifted the newspaper as though to sling it back into the drawer. But my hand suddenly froze in midair as I noticed the date.

It was a two-months-old copy of the *Globe*, and folded to one of the inside pages. I don't know why but something clicked in the old brain. Probably because it seemed strange that Trent would keep a two-months-old newspaper tucked away in his desk drawer. Particularly when he hadn't had that apartment more than a month. So I unfolded the paper and gave it the careful eye.

I learned that nylons would be back in force by the fall. And that the OPA was in for a big fight in Congress. And several other newsy tidbits that weren't worth your grandfather's old nightshirt to me.

And then, just as I was about to turn the page, I spotted it. I guess I hadn't been able to see the woods for the trees, because it was a two-column story with a head that smacked me right between the eyes. The headline read:

Long Lost U. S. Submarine
With Crew Dead
Found by navy on Tiny Pacific Island

Believed to Be One of Three That Left
Philippines With Gold and Silver
Cargo Before Jap Invasion

Another faint groan from Trent caused me to read the story at top speed. And the outstanding facts were these: A unit of the naval forces occupying the Caroline Islands had come across a U. S. submarine grounded on the coral beach of Oroluk Island. It was caught in a wedge of coral, and although the conning tower was above water, the craft was so rusted and covered with sea and shore growth it wasn't visible from more than fifty feet.

The name of the submarine and the identity of its officers and crew were being withheld by the navy department pending an investigation. However, it was stated that the undersea craft had apparently met with severe battle damage, and that by the time it had reached its final resting place all officers and crew had died from injury or battery gas poisoning. The navy department refused to state whether or not the valuable cargo had been found aboard. It was admitted, though, that it was one of the type used to evacuate gold and other valuables from the Philippines to safety when it became certain that the islands were doomed.

I read the story through twice so that all details would stick in my mind, and then I refolded the paper and slipped it back into the desk drawer. A third faint groan from Trent sent me over to the door fast. And then at that instant fifteen years were lopped off the wrong side of my life just like that! The apartment bell rang sharply.

Frozen in my tracks, I sweated blood and silently cursed with all my heart whoever was on the other side of that door. When the bell rang the second time, and longer, my mouth and throat went bone dry, and the old knees went a trifle wobbly. I did have enough sense, though, to take a couple of soft steps over to Trent, and hold my hand ready in case he started to groan too loud. Or in case he snapped out of his sleep and needed more of the same.

Four times that damn bell rang, and four times I lived through something much worse than death. And then suddenly I heard footsteps going away on the hall floor. Footsteps that clicked with me at being made by high heels. Sharp, quick taps that came faintly to my ears. In nothing flat I reached the door, eased off the lock without making a sound, and twisted the knob around and opened the door a crack. I couldn't see a thing down the hall. I took a chance and moved my head out more. And just in the nick of time, too.

I saw Beth Price step through the opened doors of the elevator and disappear from view. An instant later, the doors slid shut and the car slid downward.

For maybe three seconds, I just stood there staring at the closed elevator doors and wondering all kinds of things. Then I snapped out of my own trance. I ducked back into the apartment and removed Trent's belt from his arms. He was groaning a lot by then. Lastly I took my handkerchief and wiped the inside and outside doorknobs. Then I streaked for the fire exit stairs. Five minutes later I was in a cab, riding downtown, and wiping beads of sweat from my fevered brow.

The cabby let me off in front of the Globe Building. I rode up to the editorial rooms, and played in luck. Bill Hatch was in his little cubbyhole and pecking away at his typewriter. His brows shot high when he saw me, and he instantly pulled a bottle and two jigger glasses from his desk drawer.

'Drink this first,' he said, pouring. 'And then tell me what the hell's happened now.'

I downed it and felt much better.

'Nothing,' I said, and lighted one of his cigarettes. 'I just need a little help, that's all.'

'Don't tell me!' he mocked. 'You were so cocky last time we met. By the way, I don't think Frank Bierman loves Paula anymore.'

'What do you mean?' I barked. 'He didn't let her go?'

'On the contrary, with great relief, I imagine.' Bill grinned. 'I saw him about ten minutes ago. Paula had just left. He was saying all kinds of uncomplimentary things about womanhood and double talk. But he did stop long enough to tell me that Paula was in the clear. You should teach your darling to show more respect for cops, pal.'

'You teach her — anything.' I grinned back. 'But about this little visit. I — '

'And I think he wants to take it out on you,' Hatch went right on as though he hadn't stopped. 'At least he said he wanted to see you. Could be you're really holding out on Lieutenant Bierman, chum? Not to mention holding out on me, hmmm?'

'You're looking at a guy who is just going around in circles,' I said sadly. 'Now shut up and listen. Does your crummy rag keep a file of all the things it prints? Unusual war stories, like rescues, and stuff like that? Personal files of the guys who took part, and so forth?'

Instead of answering me, he threw back his head and had a good horse laugh, and then another drink. 'Sherlock, do you need practice and experience!' he chortled. 'Brother, are you the cute, subtle, cunning type! Take Bierman — he simply dropped in this afternoon and told me to dig it up for him, and quick.'

There was a slight sinking sensation in my belly, but I tried to ignore it. 'Dig up what?' I asked with an effort.

Hatch, the louse, let me fry for a bit while he thoroughly enjoyed every split second of it. 'I should give you three guesses, but I won't,' he finally said. 'The file on ex-Lieutenant j.g. Jordan Parsons Akerson, who quite recently stopped a knife in Paula's apartment. But ... Now, hold it! To prove what I said, that I have faith in you, pal, I didn't put the file back. Here it is.'

And there it was, right under my nose on the corner of his desk. I barely stopped myself from brushing his tapping finger away, I was that eager. Instead, I glanced down at the folder of clippings, and looked at him. 'What did Bierman want to find out?' I asked.

Hatch chuckled again and shook his head. 'He wouldn't say,' he said, getting out of his chair. 'And you won't either, of course. So nuts to you both. Help yourself while I try to earn an honest living.'

With that he walked out of the office, and I opened the folder. Ten minutes later, I had read every one of the clippings from beginning to end, and was trying to mentally slip a couple more of the cockeyed jigsaw puzzle pieces into place when Bill returned. He tried not to look curious, or even a little bit interested, but it stood out all over his face like a neon sign.

I sighed, shook my head, and swore softly. 'If Bierman learned anything from that stuff, he must be good!' I grunted, and got to my feet.

'Bierman *is* good,' Hatch said slowly, watching me. 'And so are you, liar! How's for answering some questions?'

I grinned and poured myself some more of his liquor. 'No comment to the press,' I said. 'But thanks for everything, pal. Be seeing you.'

'Now hold it, you mug,' Hatch said, and blocked my way. 'I'm your dear ever-loving pal, see? I need a story on this business bad. Listen, about Mather's finish. How's that guy Trent for a bet, huh?'

'Bierman think so?' I shot at him.

'I'm asking you,' he countered.

'Well, the answer is yes, and no,' I said, and moved past him out the door. 'Tell you which a little later. S'long.'

Bill told me in a loud voice where I could go, but I didn't. Instead I went down and out into the night-shrouded street to find a cab. I was walking toward the corner when suddenly a horn blasted right in back of me. I spun around to see twin headlights coming straight for the curb. I jumped back quickly . . . and suddenly it was curtains. My head split wide open, and my last impression before utter darkness and silence was that I was flying all over the place in small pieces.

18

My initial waking impression was that gremlins had gathered up all the little parts of me and were sewing them together with blunt needles threaded with strings of barbed wire. In plain language, I hurt like hell from head to foot. Especially the head. I knew that my eyes were open but I couldn't see a darn thing. The reason being that everything in front of me was whizzing by like streaks of light.

'See, Boss? He's coming out of it okay.'

The sudden sound of Jake's voice coming through the swirling fog was just what I needed. I mean, it burned a lot of the fog away, and the things whizzing by slowed down and began to take on definite shapes and outlines. In another couple of minutes I was able to make out White's face just a few feet from me. His brows were slightly furrowed, and his pink-tinted eyes actually held a look of

213

anxious concern.

'Try to drink this, Mr. Barnes,' his lips moved and said. 'It's some brandy. Just sip it. You had a close call, sir.'

What he said didn't register any too well on the pounding brain, but when I managed to focus on the jigger of brandy he held out, I didn't care. I took it, and let it burn its way clear down to rock bottom.

'That was hardly a sip,' White said with a faint smile. 'You want another?'

I shook my head and instantly wished I hadn't. For a second my vision was clouded by dancing pinpoints of colored flame. Then as I started to bark out the obvious question, I promptly cut myself off short. We were not in the same room where I had talked with White the last time. In fact, I was suddenly sure that we weren't even in the same building. The room was small, and comfortably enough furnished, but the two windows I could see looked out on a blank brick wall. White was seated in front of me, with the same robe covering his legs from the hips down. Jake sat to his right sipping a highball, and enjoying the surprise and befuddlement that was no doubt smeared all over my face. All that I saw in a single glance, and then brought my eyes back to White.

'Where am I, and how did I get here?' I demanded.

'In my car,' he told me. 'Jake and I brought you here. When you stumbled back and hit your head on that building entrance step, I — '

'Cut it!' I stopped him. 'I was sapped with a blackjack from behind. Listen, White, I — '

'You listen, Mr. Barnes!'

He didn't raise his voice a note, but there was something in it that made me stop automatically.

'I'm listening,' I said, grimly I hoped. 'Let's have it.'

White took a cigarette case from his pocket, flipped it open and held it out. I caught myself just in time and gestured no with my hand instead of my head. He took one and lighted up. His funny eyes were thoughtful as he let the first drag trickle out his nostrils.

'All day I've been anxious to have a talk with you, Barnes,' he suddenly started off crisply. 'You know, I told you I'd contact you when I wanted to see you. Well, twice I sent Kirby for you, and twice you refused to come. Frankly, I don't hire people to act that way.'

'And I don't hire out to come on anybody's whistle, either!'

'Well, it's water over the dam, anyway,' he said. 'And perhaps Kirby wasn't tactful. In my business, you see, I have to employ all kinds of people.'

'And just what *is* your business?' I broke in.

That struck him as funny. 'A business of making money in various ways, Mr. Barnes,' he told me when he was through laughing. 'But to get back. When I couldn't get you to come see me, I went to see you. I knew that you'd gone to the Globe Building, so I waited for you to come out. When you did, I had Jake blow the horn. I'm afraid it startled you. You jumped back, and tripped over your own feet, and hit your head on the building entrance step. I had Jake stop the car immediately and get out. You didn't seem too badly injured, so we brought you here instead of to some hospital. That's all, sir. And I deeply regret the horn startled you so you tripped and fell.'

A bare-faced lie, if I ever heard one! I had been clouted on the top of the head. For a stone step to have hit me — that would have been a neat trick by a stone step. Besides, I remembered the roof falling in while I was jumping backwards. I didn't fall until *after* the blackout. I had been sapped, and my perfect guess was by Rat Eyes Kirby. But why argue? There were much more important things.

'Okay, okay,' I said. 'Now tell me, where's here?'

'I maintain several places in the city,' White said with a smile. 'This just happens to be the one nearest where we picked you up. But let's get down to our talk, shall we? Or would you first like another drink?'

My head wanted another slug of that pre-war brandy bad, but I had a little act of my own to put on first. I took out my pen and checkbook and wrote one payable to cash for twenty-five thousand dollars.

'Here,' I said, and handed it to White. 'Now we can start from scratch with our talk. And make it good, because when I leave here I'm going to hang you high as a kite. I'm fed up with your apes gunning me around. And I'm also fed up with your cockeyed technique. Okay, talk all you want.'

'You're rather quaint, Mr. Barnes.' White smiled. 'You can walk out of here right now, and go straight to the police, and make all the silly charges you wish. Whether you are able to prove them is something else. So would be the slander suit you might have on your hands later. Take a minute and think it over. I might remind you that Jake, and Kirby, saw you accept twenty-five thousand dollars as part fee for a perfectly legal task I hired you to perform. And I'll add that I have the serial numbers of that money . . . which is now in the Hotel Biltmore safe! Well, Mr. Barnes?'

Well, Mr. Barnes was learning fast, and not feeling happy about it at all.

Frankly, I could scream my head off to Bierman and quite likely not get anyplace. I didn't know where White lived. I didn't know if that was his real name. And I didn't have a witness to swear that I had been manhandled, threatened, and finally sapped to sleep. And lastly, I didn't have any idea when, *and how*, I would get out of where I was at the moment!

'The check rides just the same!' I growled. 'We're square on that angle, anyway.'

White shook his head, smiled, and calmly tore up my check. 'I never accept checks. They must be endorsed, you know, for deposit or cashing,' he said. Then, tossing the bits onto a table at his elbow, he leaned forward a little, his face set and convincingly serious. 'Let's stop being fishwives, Mr. Barnes,' he said. 'There's too much at stake for both of us. You to make a reputation, and me to make money.'

'And so?' I murmured.

'So, two puzzling murders have been committed,' he said, leaning back in his chair and tenting his fingers. 'One yesterday, and one today. I — '

I tried to check myself, but the kid in me was too much.

'One a man you hired me to find! And the other, your lawyer!'

He nodded gravely. 'Yes, you're quite right, Mr. Barnes. One was Lieutenant Jordan Parsons Akerson. And the other was Mr. Clyde Mather.'

I managed to keep my mouth closed and my eyes in their sockets. 'You knew his real name all along?' I finally blurted out. 'Then why hire — '

A gesture of his hand stopped me. 'Not until this morning,' he said. 'That's why I sent Kirby for you.'

'Who told you?' I asked. And then the light dawned. 'Mather! And he found out from a guy named Trent?'

White smiled and arched his brows as he gestured with his two hands, palms upward. 'Mather neglected to tell me that,' he said in a flat voice. 'Perhaps from Trent. Then again, perhaps from Miss Rollins, or Miss Price, or even from Miss Grant!'

That brought me up, burning. And my action made Jake quickly put down his drink. White sat just as he was, watching me like a hawk.

'Miss Grant didn't, and remember that!' I said through my teeth.

'I apologize, Mr. Barnes,' White said smoothly. 'I was simply curious to get your reaction.'

'You got it!' I clipped. 'Miss Grant is out of this. And she stays out. Also . . . '

I cut myself off, sank back in my easy chair and stared at White with unseeing eyes. A whole lot of things were making more and more sense. A couple of things more and the Barnes might just possibly be able to slap the book shut. Well, anyway, it was a beautiful thought at the time. I enjoyed the beauty of it for a moment, and then focused my eyes on White's face, and grinned slowly.

'But you still want me to go on working for you, eh?' I grunted. And, when he nodded, 'But it wouldn't be to find Mather's killer, would it?'

His eyes seemed to blood up a little, and specks of yellow light glowed in their depths. 'What do you mean by that?' he asked, hardly moving his lips.

'Oh, not a thing,' I said airily. Then, leaning forward, I went on, 'What you *will* pay me good money for is to locate what Akerson planned to sell you for even bigger money! Right?'

Jake made sounds in his throat, but I didn't waste a glance his way. I kept my eyes fixed on White, and I was filled with a sense of almost unholy glee at the parade of expressions that took turns in his face and eyes. But after a moment, he regained control of his twitching features and smiled. He also bowed his head a mite.

'My compliments, Mr. Barnes,' he said. 'That, I did not really suspect. My answer is yes. And you can name your own price.'

I grinned because I was feeling wonderful. More wonderful than I'd felt since Paula's last kiss. 'So Clyde Mather beat you to it twice, eh?' I said, watching him.

'I beg your pardon?' He frowned.

'Clyde Mather,' I said, and swung into my act. 'He killed Akerson for what

Akerson had to sell you. And then . . . '

'Don't be stupid, Barnes!'

'Am I being?' I grinned at him. Then I threw the fast one. 'Mather had a key to Miss Grant's apartment!'

It was a ball, way outside. The lug didn't so much as bat an eyelash. He seemed to know that choice bit, too. He even chuckled a little. Anyway, it sounded like a chuckle.

'So Mather killed Akerson?' he purred. 'Very interesting!'

'It might be to the police,' I said. 'Also, why Mather was shot!'

White was still smiling at me.

'And why was Mather shot, Mr. Barnes?' he asked quietly. I was being nagged by the feeling that I was out over my depth, but it was whole hog or nothing.

'Because he decided to work for peanuts no longer!' I shot at him. 'Mather decided to go into business for himself. And he lost his life in the deal. Check?'

He didn't reply. He half closed his eyes, fixed them on a point just over my head, and paddled his tented fingertips against each other. I gave him a few seconds, and then on the spur of the instant decided to add something else to my little speech.

'And it would certainly *look* crazy, wouldn't it, for a man to plunk out twenty-five thousand dollars to find somebody he already knew was dead? Or about to be made dead?'

White slowly opened his eyes and lowered his hands.

'You're an utter damn fool, Barnes, to even think that, much less state it to my face!' he said in a voice that was like gravel going down a chute. Then, with a quick change of voice tone, he said, 'But I can see how you possibly might think it. But you're wrong, and we're getting way off the subject. We were talking about you finding for me . . . for a price, of course . . . what Akerson had when he was killed.'

'By Mather,' I added, grinning.

He started to get mad, and then shrugged it off with a sigh. 'Very well, we'll assume that Mather murdered Akerson,' he said. 'But Mather in turn was murdered, and I still haven't got what

I want. Tell me, who do you think has it?'

I was enjoying things again, and I let my grin spread. 'I haven't the faintest idea,' I told him.

White held up his left hand with the fingers extended, and then with the forefinger of his right he started to count them off. 'Miss Rita Rollins, for one,' he said. 'Trent for another. Miss Beth Price for a third. And . . . Miss Grant for a fourth!'

'Hold it!' I grated. 'I told you — '

'Shut up!' came his voice like a whip. 'Mather had lunch with Miss Grant a short time before he was killed. I'm not accusing, Barnes, I'm stating a fact!'

It was a fact, so I was forced to let it ride. 'And the fifth?' I asked sullenly.

'Is you, Mr. Barnes. Though somehow, I doubt that much.'

'Thanks for the doubt,' I said with a forced laugh. 'You had me worried there for a moment.'

'Believe me, you have plenty of cause for worry, Barnes!' he said in a steely voice that actually did startle me. 'I never play games I can't win. I also make my own rules. You understand me?'

'Maybe I do,' I said. 'So what?'

'So get it for me,' he said, 'and one hundred thousand dollars, in addition to what I've already paid you, is yours when you do.'

'Not a bad fee,' I murmured. Then looking at his sober face, I asked, 'And how much if I come up with Akerson's killer, and Mather's killer, too?'

'Not one red cent,' he said. 'I'm not interested. But *if* you do, I'm sure the newspaper publicity will be reward enough.'

'I wonder,' I murmured, and looked at the lump that still showed over Jake's eye. 'Satisfaction isn't a bad reward at times.'

White caught my look, and the ghost of a smile passed along his lips. 'Probably not,' he murmured. Then, holding out a jigger of brandy, 'Well, let's drink to your success . . . and to mine.'

I drank to my success only. And about five seconds later, I wished I hadn't drunk at all. There was suddenly a crazy pounding in my ears. White's face got smaller and smaller. I swore at him but the words didn't come off my lips. I tried to get up but I could only make it halfway. The last conscious thought I had was that I was leaving the place exactly the way I had arrived. Out cold!

19

I was just dimly conscious of a hand shaking my shoulder, and of somebody's voice rumbling in my ears. However, I was too sleepy, and too blah, to care a damn about anything. Presently, though, the shoulder-shaking became a little rough, and the rumbling voice booming.

'Come on, mister! Go on home and sleep it off. You can't do it here. Come on, wake up!'

A sharp slap that left my cheek stinging pulled me up out of the fuzzy-wuzzy well of semi-consciousness and pried open my eyes. I found myself sprawled out on a bench in some kind of a park, and bending over me was one of New York's finest. I saw his buttons and police shield in the faint glow of a park lamp a couple of dozen yards away. I blinked a couple of times, recognized my immediate surroundings as part of Central Park, and sat up. The cop, the lamp, and the night-shadowed park spun around at terrific speed. I felt myself keeling over, and I would have spilled off the bench onto the gravel walk if the cop hadn't caught and steadied me.

'Easy, mack,' the cop said. Then, 'My God! Watcha been drinking? Antifreeze?'

'A Mickey Finn,' I managed to mumble. 'A double one. Where the hell am I?'

'Central Park,' the cop confirmed. 'I been letting you sleep it off for an hour now. But the lieutenant will be coming by soon, see? A Mickey? Who slipped it to you?'

I didn't answer right away. First I forced my eyes to focus on my wrist-watch, and saw that it was quarter after seven. Then I stood up slowly and sucked a lot of air into my lungs. That helped a whole lot. Only nine-tenths of me continued to feel awful. Anyway, I was ready and willing to go on living some more.

'A louse,' I said, trying to grin. 'It'll be my turn next time. But thanks, Officer. I guess I can navigate under my own steam now. Which way to the nearest exit, where I can get a cab?'

'Just around that curve,' the cop said, pointing to the left. 'But are you sure you're — Hey! Just a minute!'

One hand of the law closed over my arm, and the other hand whipped in under my jacket and came out with my gun. For the first second I could only gape at it stupidly. And then I seethed at top heat as I pictured White, or Kirby, or maybe Jake, slipping it into its holster as they carted me away. It certainly hadn't been in its holster when I was talking to White.

'That's mine!' I finally blurted out foolishly.

'Is it, now?' the cop said, and broke the gun. 'Hah! No slugs, eh?'

Yes, my gun was empty, and I began to feel more and more foolish.

'I'm Gerry Barnes, a private investigator,' I said. 'Here. Here's identification. I'm — '

I stopped short because by then I had my wallet out and was fingering through it for my card, and not finding it right away because somebody else had gone through it quite recently! When I did find it I showed it to the cop with a couple of other things.

'So you're Barnes, huh?' he grunted, and gave me back my gun. 'I read a piece about you starting up. Some start you seem to be making. A Mickey, and no slugs in your gun. Better get some, Barnes. The tough lads in this town don't scare worth a damn.'

I assured him I'd do just that, and started walking quickly away, my face on fire because I knew he was standing there laughing at me and wagging his head. What I had to live down if he told the boys in the precinct room!

Anyway, I got out of the park as fast as my slightly shaky legs would take me, eventually got a cab, and rode it straight to my apartment. Two good drinks, a cold needle shower, and a complete change of clothes from the skin out, revived my health if it didn't my spirits. By then it was eight o'clock, and for the first time I remembered my date with Paula. I called the Biltmore, only to learn that she had checked out. I waited for her to be paged around the place, and then hung up and dialed her apartment phone. I hung up again when I heard the bell sound for the umpteenth time.

I was not so sorry I'd been unable to reach Paula. I had other things to do. So I did the first one. I called Rita, and miracle of miracles, I found her in at that early-evening hour. And all alone, she told me.

'I want to see you, baby,' I told her. 'Right away. No, not at your place. Can you grab a cab and be in my office in fifteen minutes?'

There was a long pause, and I got all set to argue.

'Well, if you want, darling,' her voice came over the wire. 'But it would be much cozier down here. I've scotch and rye. And, also, I'm not dressed.'

'Then get dressed!' I snapped. 'Maybe later on the scotch, but right now it's business. I want your help on something, Rita.'

'Oh, well, that's different!' she said, and laughed. 'I'm putting on my bra right

232

now. Fifteen minutes, lover!'

I hung up and grinned at the phone until the parade of thoughts turned around and came back. I let the grin fade from my face, and went into the bedroom. Eight minutes later I was in my office. And five minutes after that Rita came sailing in looking as though she'd just stepped out of one of the better Madison Avenue shops. She twirled around once, and then danced over for the kiss, and got it.

'Don't I look nice, darling?' she cooed, and clung to me. 'I was just hoping you'd call, and you did. Oh, Gerry, darling, I — '

Her voice had gone up the scale, and I could feel her nails through the cloth of my jacket sleeves.

'Cut!' I said, and pushed her arms down. Then, softening it with a grin, 'Business before pleasure.'

She pouted but backed up and sat down in a chair.

'Why the hell don't people change that around once in a while!' she said. Then, with a little laugh, 'But Rita can wait.

What is it, lover? How can I help you?'

I didn't answer. I went over to the safe, opened it up, and took out the sealed envelope she had given me for safekeeping.

As I carried it back to the desk, her eyes narrowed, and then opened wide in innocent puzzlement. 'What's the matter, Gerry? Don't you want to keep it for me any longer?'

I didn't answer that one, either. I sat tapping the sealed envelope with a thumb and looking at her. And thinking a whole lot of things I sincerely didn't want to think.

'Maybe it isn't legal, Rita, I don't know,' I presently said slowly. 'Maybe you can even sue, and get every dime I have. I don't know about that, either. But I'm going to open this right now!'

My eyes never left her face as I talked, and I guess I witnessed the expression of every emotion possible in a woman. But, believe it or not, the last was cool, almost icy, indifference.

'All right, Mr. Smart Detective, go ahead and open it!'

Rita's voice shook, and her black eyes blazed. I tried to think fast for some way to wiggle out of it with a laugh for us both. But I couldn't think of any. Feeling cheaper than I had ever felt before, I slit open the envelope and dumped its contents onto the desk.

'And take a *good* look!' came Rita's hoarse voice as I stared miserably at the collection of stuff. 'Two hundred dollars in War Bonds! My birth certificate. My USO card. My Red Cross thing. My saving account book. My . . . Oh, the hell with you! See for yourself!'

I did, and what I would have bet my life on wasn't there. Slowly I put the stuff back into the envelope, and then handed her the lot.

'Sorry,' I said. Then, trying a grin, 'I'm sorry as hell, baby. I — '

Right about then the lightning struck, and sat me up straight with my mouth hanging open a little. Rita regarded me with her interpretation of scorn.

'Now what, Master Mind?'

I think I suddenly hated the gal a little.

'Just a minor item,' I said evenly. 'Why

the hell get so steamed up? Because you know damn well what it was I was looking for! *Isn't that true?*'

On the last, I leaned way toward her with my chin out and my eyes cold and steady. She glared at me for an instant, and then the damn little wench stuck her own face forward and kissed me.

'Certainly, lover mine!' she purred. 'But you've never asked me to help you, until now. Always you've been rushing off to darling Paula.'

I sank back in my chair, a flabbergasted guy. 'Well, I'll be damned!'

The daze still held me, so Rita was on my lap before I could stop her. 'You look so funny, lover!' she giggled under my nose. 'Does it surprise you as much as all that? Remember last night when you made that crummy mink coat crack? I wanted to tell you all about Jord Akerson then. Oh, you louse. I could kill you for what you were thinking a few minutes ago!'

Instead of killing me, she kissed me again, and then slid off my lap and back to her chair. I stared at her, and shook my head like I was waiting for the nine count. Then I impulsively opened the desk drawer and took out the bottle and two glasses.

'A quick one first,' I said, pouring. 'And then you're going to do a hell of a lot of talking, Miss Rollins.'

She laughed, downed hers in a gulp, and laughed again. 'Just talking, Mr. Barnes?' she said coyly. Then, with a quick change to the serious, she said, 'But you must be damn clever, darling. How did you find out? Oh! Did that simpering sop, Clyde Mather, tell you at Trent's apartment this morning?'

I shook my head slowly. 'No,' I said. 'I found out a couple of things, and then guessed there was a map. But you do the talking. Begin with when you met Akerson. Where, and how?'

'It was a couple of days after I met Trent,' she said. 'And that was at Beth Price's party. He and Harry were at the bar right after my number. Harry introduced me, and he seemed a nice enough guy. Anyway, the three of us went on a little toot. Harry had money he wanted to spend. We had fun.'

'No doubt,' I said dryly. 'Go on.'

She shot me a hurt look before lowering her eyes. For a second I expected to see real tears. 'You could have made everything so different, Gerry,' she said so low I almost didn't get it. Anyway, I ignored it.

'Then what?' I prompted. 'Did Akerson tell you his story then?'

'No, it was a week or so later. Harry wasn't with us, and Jord got pretty drunk and troublesome. To get his mind off things, I tried to get him to talk about his war experiences.' She paused and looked up at me, with a slightly scornful smile. 'Sometimes when you're high, your silent heroes do a lot of talking about themselves, you know.'

'Yeah, I know,' I said, and let it rest there.

'Well, I got him started,' Rita went on. 'After a while, he was pretty bitter about it all. Hated the navy and the guys in it. Particularly the high-stripers. Anyway, he got boasting that his service in the navy was going to pay off big. Maybe even in millions, he said. Boy, he was plastered!'

'So you said,' I grunted at her pause. 'What was his story?'

She looked at me with a peculiar expression I couldn't fathom. 'If you know about the map, then you must know the story,' she said. 'So why ask?'

'Part I know, part I can guess,' I said. 'Akerson was shot down on Oroluk in the Carolines, and three months later was sighted and rescued by a navy PBY on recce patrol. That's a matter of record. This part isn't, yet. While on Oroluk, and keeping out of sight of the Japs, he discovered a long-lost U. S. submarine, unreported since leaving Manila in early Forty-two with a cargo of Philippine government gold and silver and stuff. The sub after a battle had been beached, or had washed ashore on Oroluk. Time and tide had covered it with stuff, so it was only by chance Akerson found it. Right so far?'

'Just about,' Rita said. 'His gunner and he found it together when they were hunting for food. He said the gunner died later from injuries received in the crash and he buried him. I wonder, though. There was something queer about Akerson.'

'Very queer!' I agreed, and dropped it. 'Anyway, Akerson took the gold, and maybe the other stuff, ashore a little at a time, and buried it. Maybe the little birds told him he was going to live out the war.'

'He did say something like that to me,' Rita broke in. 'He said he dreamed every night that he was being rescued. And that he felt absolutely sure that he would be sooner or later.'

'So he drew a map, with X marking the spot,' I said. Then, quickly, 'Did you ever see it?'

'Yes, that night. But that was the only time I ever saw it. And he wasn't so drunk he let me see anything I could remember. Just some crazy pencil marks was all I saw.'

'Well, that's the end of my guessing,' I said. 'The rest is all blank. How did he come to contact a guy by the name of White?'

Rita's eyes widened, and her lips formed a circle. 'Oh, so that was his name? Jord would never tell me that. He would only say that he knew somebody that was going to pay him heavy sugar for the map. Somebody who had the money to finance a trip to Oroluk, just as soon as it wouldn't look suspicious. I . . . Gerry, I'm scared. I'm scared as hell!'

She suddenly looked it, and I asked her why. 'Why? Isn't it obvious?' she cried.

'No!' I said. 'But before you make it clear, answer me this! How did you know Akerson was dead, and his gold map missing?'

She just looked at me for a long minute. And then she began to cry, so softly there was hardly a sound.

I apologized, I swore at her to shut up, and I offered her a drink. The drink she accepted. Then she cried some more. 'Oh, Gerry . . . Gerry!'

That's all I could get out of her until she'd finished with her tears, and another drink.

'Trent came back again after you left last night,' she said in a dull voice. 'He'd been expecting to see Jord all day, but hadn't. When he read about the man in

Paula's apartment, he went to the morgue. He told me it was Akerson. He practically accused me of killing Jord and stealing the map. Don't you see now? He probably still thinks so. And so does this White, if that's his name. Can't you see, Gerry? My life may not be worth a nickel this minute!'

I looked at her plenty perplexed, ignoring the pretty-please in her tear-filled eyes.

'You lied this morning, Rita,' I told her bluntly. 'You didn't try to see Willis about any contract. Willis told me he called it off yesterday morning when you blew into his office cockeyed, and demanded triple the money he was offering or you wouldn't sing in his crummy joint. Why?'

'That fancy pants!' Rita fairly spat out. 'I always hated the place, and especially Willis. God, how that eel can paw! Sure I told him what I thought. I didn't care a damn then. Jord Akerson said he wanted me to leave as soon as he collected. And why not? Damn it, I'm not getting any younger!'

She was so close to the point of flying

apart in small pieces that I hesitated. And then I went ahead with it anyway. 'It was Trent, wasn't it, who tried to get in this morning, and later did?' I asked. 'And Mather who phoned and got you away?'

Rita started to form words with her lips, gave it up, and started again. 'Clyde Mather phoned, yes,' she said. 'He said it was important, and would I meet him in Child's on Fourteenth right away. I did, and all he wanted was to offer me a contract to sing at a club he said he part-owned. I told him I'd think it over.'

'But why did you tell me — ' I began.

'Good grief, Gerry, can't you realize why now? I just wanted to keep out of things happening, and a lot had. Trent, you say? Hey! Maybe somebody thought Jord had given me the map before he was killed! Gerry, know what I think? I think Harry Trent lied to me last night about *not* seeing Jord Akerson yesterday. I — I — '

She stumbled over the rest. Then, suddenly, she leaped to her feet, stamped them, and hurled her purse to the floor. Just like Paula.

'Damn it!' she blazed. 'A woman is nice to a couple of ex-service men, and look what happens! She's practically up to her ears in murder! Damn all you men, anyway!'

Suddenly my office phone rang.

20

To be truthful, I jumped a couple of inches myself when the darn thing rang. And as for Rita, she went white as a sheet, and against that background her red, red lips and her jet-black eyes gave her one hell of a ghastly appearance. She started to pick her purse up off the floor, checked herself, and stood there staring at the phone as though it was a cobra ready to strike.

'Relax, baby,' I said, and picked up the thing and announced myself.

The voice I heard was quite a surprise to me.

'Barnes, this is Trent. What do you want to see me about?'

'See you about?' I echoed.

'Yes,' he said. 'Your message I just got. Asking me to come down to your office. What about?'

I took a couple of seconds to think that over and figure something out. I certainly hadn't sent Trent any message to come to see me.

'When did you get my message?' I stalled for time.

'Just now. It was sent up from downstairs. I called to see if you were in your office.'

'Well, here I am,' I said slowly. 'Matter of fact, I would like a couple of words with you, Trent. Can you come down?'

'Right away,' he replied instantly. 'And there's a couple of things I want to see you about, too! Goodbye!'

He hung up, and so did I, thoughtfully. The tone of voice had been a dead giveaway. I mean, Harry Trent was suddenly one scared guy!

'Harry Trent's coming down here?'

Rita's strained-voice question jerked me away from my thoughts. I looked at her and nodded.

'Yes,' I said. 'Says he wants to see me about a couple of things. I want to see him, too.'

Rita bit her lower lip and made as though to say something. Then she checked herself and bent over and picked up her purse.

'Darling, be careful, won't you?' she said, and stepped close. I thought of all the lumps on my head and winced.

'Don't worry, the Barnes always is,' I lied cheerfully. 'You got an idea why Trent wants to see me?'

'No, no, I haven't,' she said, and shook her raven locks violently. 'I just — I just feel funny, that's all. God, but I wish Beth had never thrown that party!'

'Make a guess, baby,' I said suddenly. 'Who do you suppose has the damn gold map?'

She puckered up her brows and bit some more on her lower lip. Hard enough to draw blood in another minute.

'I can't even make a guess,' she said slowly after a long pause. Then, even more thoughtfully, 'Do you know, Gerry, I wonder if Jord Akerson hadn't completed the deal before he was murdered.'

'No, that's out,' I told her. 'Just a few hours ago, the mysterious Mr. White offered me a hundred grand to get that map for him.'

The mere mention of money always did make Rita's eyes dance, and this time was no exception to prove the rule. 'A hundred thousand dollars, Gerry? Gee, I hope you find it, darling!'

I shrugged, and then came another thought. 'Did Clyde Mather's name ever enter into the talks between you and Akerson and Trent?' I asked. Then I added, 'Trent of course knew that you knew, didn't he?'

'Yes, I'm sure he did, though neither of us ever mentioned it. But toward the last, Harry was acting awful damn jealous of Jord. But Clyde Mather's name was never mentioned that I remember. What do you think about Clyde, anyway, Gerry? He was a terrible drip, but hell — to get murdered!'

'Yeah, it was sort of tough on Mather,' I grunted. 'However, he was much in the picture.'

Rita looked faintly surprised, and then suddenly her eyes really went wide. She even put fingertips to her partly opened mouth, as though to stop words that were coming forth. I looked at her hard.

'Spill it!' I said. 'What were you going to say?'

'Clyde!' she said as though it hurt to get the word out. 'Didn't it say in the newspaper that the police didn't know how Akerson's murderer got into Paula's apartment? Well, Clyde was crazy about Paula, and I know that Paula liked him a lot. Well . . . '

'Shut up, you fool!' I blazed, and almost let her have it. 'Paula's — '

'Shut up, yourself!' she screamed back at me. 'I don't mean what *you* mean, you heel! Paula's okay. But here's something you probably *don't* know! Clyde Mather *did* have a key to Paula's apartment at one time. Over a year ago. He got it from Beth Price to put flowers in Paula's apartment just before she got back from a trip out west. Beth had been using her apartment. That's true, Gerry. I know, because I helped Clyde pick out the flowers!' And then to add to things, she started to cry.

'Oh, cut it out!' I growled, and gave her my handkerchief. 'You better go home, baby, and get some sleep. Besides, Trent will be here any minute. You don't want to see him, do you?'

That did it. She wiped off the final tear and tossed my handkerchief on the desk. 'Not that louse, no!' she said viciously. Then, coming close, 'And I don't want to go home, either. Dammit, darling, I'm afraid. I'm scared stiff, honest to God. Can't — can't you get me a hotel room or something?'

She should have asked for the moon, too. I looked at her and was suddenly a little sorry for her. She really was scared, and fighting it hard. I made a sudden decision, crossed my fingers, and prayed that it wouldn't get my head placed on the chopping block. I mean, I pulled out my apartment key and gave it to her.

'Go to my place,' I said. 'Make yourself comfortable, but don't answer the door ring until you're sure it's me, see? We'll talk about what to do later.'

She took the key and pressed it between her two hands as though it was the most wonderful thing in the world. She lifted her face and smiled at me through new tears. 'You darling, darling!'

she whispered, and smeared my cheeks with those new tears.

'Beat it!' I said before I could change my mind. 'Scram out before Trent gets here.'

Rita scrammed, and I sat down at the desk for a little think session. But first I picked up my handkerchief and removed various and sundry lipstick marks from my face. Then I postponed the thinking again while I tried Paula's number. Still no answer, and the little lumps of worry-lead began to move around in the belly.

Then the door opened, and Trent came in. He was out of uniform and wearing civvies. Nice one, too — nice cut. He was also wearing something new to me on his face. A worried expression that you might even take for fear. When I noted that, I relaxed, and even gave him a smile.

'Sit down, Trent,' I said, and waved a hand. 'So there really is something on your mind, eh?'

'Plenty, Barnes!' he said grimly. 'But first, what did you want to see me about?'

I offered him a smoke, and held my

lighter for both of us. 'I didn't want to see you when you phoned,' I told him. 'I didn't even send you any message.'

He looked at me as though I'd told him he was the father of quintuplets. Then the dumbfoundedness faded, and baffled fear really got hold of him. 'Look, Barnes, I'm in one hell of a jam. Oh, I know that you have more dough than I ever hope to see, but just the same I'll pay you all I possibly can, if you'll help me out.'

That was interesting, and about to become more interesting. 'How?'

He started to tell me, but seemed to change his mind.

'How much do you know about the man killed in your woman's apartment?' he asked me instead. 'And that fellow, Mather, shot this afternoon?'

'I know a lot,' I told him evenly. 'One of the items being that you told Lieutenant Bierman I threatened Mather in your place this morning. Which was a lie, Trent!'

'I guess I was pretty sore at you, Barnes,' he mumbled. 'That wasn't any love tap you laid on my chin. And that

God damn fool, Bierman, was practically accusing me of shooting Mather. Christ! I was the one who phoned him!'

'So he told me,' I said. 'But about this jam you find yourself in. Rather, how can I help you? So that you can skip details, I know about Akerson, and Oroluk Island, and the gold map, and the built-up deal with a guy named White. By the way, how did you learn about White being interested in such things? You know him?'

'No.' He shook his head. 'Mather told me. At a party where I met Mather, we got talking about treasures and ship cargoes lost in the war. He said he knew a man who would finance a salvaging expedition, if it could be proved worth the cost. Well, I . . . '

He stopped and looked at me. The guy was about ready to bust out in tears, he was so suddenly sad and ashamed. I just looked back at him and let him feel that way.

'I was in Akerson's torpedo squadron,' he went on talking. 'But I didn't get to know him well before he got busted out. I met him again a month or so ago, and

. . . Well, what the hell, he seemed a nice enough guy to me. Anyway, we barged around some together. Then one night he told me about that gold submarine, and what he'd done. He didn't give me a look at the map, though. He — ' Trent stopped again for a look at me. 'You're following me, aren't you?' he said. 'I mean, you know all about what I'm — '

'Could be I'm way ahead of you,' I said. 'But go on. No, let me for a change. You remembered your talk with Mather, and told Akerson. How did Akerson contact White? Through Mather?'

'Yes. He gave me a letter I gave to Mather. It had a couple of newspaper clippings that — '

'One, the story of finding the long-lost sub,' I broke in. 'And one that was the story of Akerson's rescue by a PBY from Oroluk Island.'

Trent seemed to shiver a little.

'Christ, you do find out things, don't you?'

'I find out lots of things,' I assured him smugly. 'Was it Akerson's idea, or yours, to change Akerson's name to Jordan, and make him hard to reach?'

'Both,' he said. 'I didn't feel too sure about Mather. Besides ... Well, to tell you the God's truth, Barnes, I pulled out of the thing after I'd given Akerson's letter to Mather. After thinking it over, I decided that I didn't want any part of that kind of a deal. I told Akerson to count me out. He got sore, and we had a battle over it. I never saw him or heard from him again after that. And that was four or five days before he was murdered.'

I let him wait a couple of moments before I spoke. 'But you *did* see him again, Trent.'

It was practically like slapping him in the mush. He ducked back and instinctively brought up his guard for the second smack. 'What the hell do you mean?' he wanted to know.

'Dead,' I said. 'At the morgue last night. Right?'

'Oh, that!' he said, and you should have caught the relief. 'Yes, that's true. When I read about it in the papers — the little bit they did print — the clothes sounded like Akerson's. I ... Hell, I'd *known* the guy!

Anyway, I went down and got the guy there to let me take a look. A couple of others were taking a look, too. Two old women. The guy didn't ask our names, and I didn't tell him mine. And when I recognized Akerson, I didn't say I did, either.'

'Why?'

Trent looked at me as though that was really stupid. 'I was out of the deal,' he said. 'And I was damn well going to stay out. Murder's not my dish!'

'But this morning you changed your mind, eh?'

'Eh?' he echoed back at me blankly.

'When you went down to Rita's, and messed up her place looking for the gold map you thought was there!' I said sharply.

His face went all shades, but mostly black. He jumped to his feet, and I got set for the swing that didn't come. 'Hell, you're not as smart as I thought you were!' he snarled at me. 'Like hell I did!'

'Skip it, and sit down,' I said with a gesture. 'Even smart people can guess wrong. So skip it. You're in a jam, you were saying?'

The wind went right out of his sails, which was proof enough.

'Yes,' he said in a shaky voice. 'This guy White, whoever the hell he is, thinks I've got the map!'

'Yeah?' from me. 'He tell you?'

'No. But early this evening I answered my apartment bell, and got knocked cold. When I came to my belt was on the floor beside me, and my handkerchief over my face. I'd been searched, and so had the whole apartment. By an expert, too. I could tell.'

'Anything missing?' I asked, straight-faced.

'No. But the place had been gone over good.'

'So what?' I grunted. And then I couldn't help adding, 'What makes you think it was White?'

'Mather,' he came right back at me.

'Come again?' I asked, because I didn't get that one.

He hesitated a moment to make sure the words came out right. 'What's White look like?' he suddenly asked.

'I don't know,' I lied. 'Why?'

'I've seen a big guy two or three times today,' Trent told me as a worried frown worked his brows. 'I'm damn sure, now, I've been followed. Last time I saw him was when the cops let me leave Mather's apartment. Look, do you suppose Mather got his because he was holding out on White? Or White thinks I got Mather, and I have the map?'

'You think Mather had the map?' I countered with the question.

'Do you?' he came right back at me, his eyes glued to mine.

I started to answer that one, but thought better of it, and let it ride. There was a more important point that I wanted to get straight.

'Did Mather see you again after you had given him Akerson's letter?' I asked.

'No,' he answered after a faint pause. 'I wasn't in town. I had to go down to Washington to attend to something. I didn't get back until yesterday morning. You can check!'

So that was that? Unable to contact

Akerson because Trent was out of town, I had been called in by White to do the hunting, on Mather's suggestion? Or had Mather been more in White's mind than Akerson when we had had our little talk?

One thing was certain. Pink Eyes White certainly hadn't mentioned Mather's name to me.

'There's only one thing I know!' Trent broke into my thought session. 'And it's that I'm in the middle of two murders I didn't have anything to do with. White seems to be after me because he thinks I have that damn map. And Bierman is after me for Christ knows what! Look, Barnes, I've come down here and voluntarily told you *everything* I know. I want you to help me so's I can stay *out* of this lousy mess!'

21

I took my time. I studied Trent's face carefully, and I mulled over half a dozen thoughts and things that occurred to me. Then presently I shrugged, and made a little half-gesture with one hand.

'Considering this and that, Trent,' I said slowly, 'just how do you figure I can help you?'

He leaned way forward in his chair, his face tense. 'Easy enough, Barnes,' he said. 'Look, I've done all the fighting I want to do in my life. So I don't want to wake up some morning dead like Mather, or Akerson, just because White, or somebody, has a mad idea about me. I've told you all I know. Everything, see?'

I just looked at him and waited.

'The God's truth, Barnes!' he exclaimed. 'I want to leave this damn town. I only came here for a visit, anyway. But I don't want the cops all over the country hunting for me just because that dope,

Bierman, isn't convinced.'

'Bierman is no dope,' I told him truthfully. 'But go on. What do you expect me to do?'

'See Bierman and point out to him that I couldn't possibly have had anything to do with either murder, or that damn missing map!' Trent said almost savagely. Then, with a half-shrug and a twist of his head, he went on, 'Sure, I'm admitting that I told Akerson what Mather told me, and that I took Akerson's letter to him. But — but, hell, that's no crime! I — why, I was just doing a favor, for a war service buddy. Don't you see?'

No, I couldn't see. A red haze was filming my eyes, and it was suddenly sort of difficult to breathe. I felt my hands doubling into fists, but I forced myself to relax. I even forced myself not to look at the so-inviting point of the louse's jaw. And lastly, I forced myself to count ten silently.

'A fine favor, Trent!' the words finally came. 'A damn fine favor to those poor devils who died trying to transport that

261

gold to safety! Hell, I ought to knock your brains out!'

I really meant what I said, and no doubt it showed quite clearly in my eyes. Trent came up on his feet quickly and moved around in back of his chair.

'Now wait a minute, Barnes!' he said. 'That's not the point. Sure those poor guys died, but if Akerson hadn't found the stuff, the Japs probably would have. And listen, I don't owe a thing to anybody. I risked my life enough times. I killed my share of Japs. I served my country, and — '

And right then, my office phone bell startled me for the second time. I was still gazing at Trent's chin, so the phone rang twice before I picked it up. And when I did, I heard a voice at the other end that I was really glad to hear. Paula's.

'Hello, you! Thanks for the lovely dinner. What do you want to see Beth and me about?'

'What do you mean, see you and Beth?' I asked, startled. 'Where are you, anyway?'

'Downstairs in the lobby,' she said.

Then, more sharply, 'Are you drunk, Gerry? This isn't a gag, is it?'

'Damn right, it isn't!' I barked, as an uneasy feeling began to seep through my chest. 'Answer my question. What about you and Beth? Who told you I wanted to see you?'

'Why *you*, so we thought!' she replied in an odd-sounding voice. 'Beth's date fell through, so she came back and met me at the Biltmore. We waited until eight for you, and then went in and started eating. About fifteen minutes ago there was a phone call for me. Somebody said you wanted to see us both at your office. And then he hung up. I don't know *all* your friends, darling, so Beth and I took a taxi. But I got thinking on the way. So I'm phoning. You really didn't want to see us?'

'No,' I said. Then changed it in the same breath. 'Yes! Come on up right away!'

'Okay, Gerry, be seeing you,' she said, and hung up.

Trent was over by the door when I pushed the phone away. His face looked mad, but I could tell he was still scared inside.

'Then it's no deal?' he asked with an effort.

'No deal!' I told him curtly. Then, just like they do in the movies, 'And I'm warning you not to leave town, Trent!'

His lips tightened, and I expected to hear him ask me who the hell I thought I was. He didn't.

'Maybe a couple of others shouldn't, either,' he said.

And the look he gave me just before he ducked out the door was another little surprise in my full life. Damned if the guy didn't mean me for one!

I mulled that over for a moment or two and got a laugh out of it. And I also got sore, too. The market price on that map at the moment was a hundred thousand dollars. And even to somebody with money, a hundred grand is not to be shrugged off. Certainly not to a man like White; not to mention Rat Eyes Kirby and those two apes.

Anyway, it was all food for thought, but I wasn't able to partake of much. The door opened and Paula and Beth trooped in. Seeing Paula did the aching head an awful lot of good, and my cares and worries went away for a moment. But only a moment. He was a dope. A forgetful guy. Paula spotted the bottle and the two glasses still on the desk. Particularly the glass that had the lipstick smear on the rim. She slowed to a stop and smiled sweetly.

'Did you get her out in time, darling? Or is she hiding in the johnny? Such an appropriate place, too!'

'You can go to hell!' I said. 'Rita was here, and in a bad way. She needed a drink, and so did I. So what? Sit down. You too, Beth!'

If there was a nasty crack coming up out of Paula's lovely throat, it died before I could hear it. She gave me a keen look, and the nasty bittersweetness went away and hid. She sat down, and so did Beth.

'Progress is not so hot, huh, Gerry?' Paula asked.

'*Progress* is getting all bitched up!' I said bluntly. 'Now, tell me again what you told me over the phone.'

265

She did, and without adding anything. Listening to her, the uneasy feeling abated somewhat. I thought I began to see the light. In short, White was employing a cockeyed way of needling me into earning that hundred thousand in a hurry. Learning that I was in my office, he had arranged for the suspects, to *him*, to come to see me. Just what he expected me to get out of the wholesale interview was his secret. It certainly wasn't mine. For me, the case was galloping down the home stretch. I hoped! Anyway, I didn't need any of White's screwy help.

'Then you knew nothing about the call?' Paula asked when I just sat there thinking my own thoughts.

'No,' I said. 'But I know what it's all about. What about your visit with Bierman? He get rough?'

'The gentleman is a gentleman,' she said, and grinned. 'He was courtesy itself. But I'm afraid I wasn't much help to him. I simply wouldn't please him by confessing to everything. In fact, he did seem quite annoyed when I was unable to even make a guess what in hell it was all about.

But I did guess that he isn't too fond of you! Incidentally, I met Bill Hatch coming away. He mentioned that you weren't exactly cooperating.'

'Nuts!' I said to that. 'I'm having the devil's own job trying to cooperate with myself. Bierman say anything else?'

'No.' She shook her head. Then, with a half-look at Beth Price, she went on, 'But there is something else, Gerry. That Luger you gave me for a souvenir — I can't find it. It isn't there in the drawer.'

Something that could have been a cold slimy snake coiled itself about my heart. 'What do you mean?' I asked foolishly. 'When did you look?'

'This evening,' she told me. 'Shortly after I saw Bierman. I checked out, and moved back to the apartment. Just before I went down to be stood up by you at the Biltmore, I thought of the gun, and took a look. It wasn't there. I — *Gerry!*'

It was so sharp and clear, I blinked. 'Yes?'

Paula's face had paled a little, and she had to lick her luscious lips before she spoke. 'Gerry! Could the police get a passkey from the apartment building manager?'

'Sure,' I said slowly.

Then ice-water rose up in me to the neckline. Had Bierman during his first search of the apartment seen Paula's gun? And then gone back for it, and not found it, after Clyde Mather was killed? In other words ... I refused to let myself think anymore along that line. I made a sudden decision. Without offering Paula or Beth a drink, I popped the bottle and glasses back in the desk drawer. I pushed it shut, and stood up.

'Maybe you put it someplace else and forgot,' I said. 'Did you hunt all around?'

'No, because it should have been in that drawer,' she said firmly. 'Besides, it was almost seven. I decided to tell you about it right away.'

'Well, we'll go really look, and now,' I said. Then, as another disturbing thought crowded in with the others, 'I had you paged at the Biltmore a little after eight. They said you weren't there.'

'But that's not true!' Beth Price burst out for the first time. 'We were, weren't we, darling? The page boy just didn't come into the dining room, I guess.'

I shrugged, and then caught Paula's steady look. She wasn't pale anymore. Definitely not! The lightning in her eyes was winding up to throw curves.

'You wouldn't be thinking anything, would you, Mr. Heel?' she asked, tight-lipped.

'It can wait until this business is all through,' I snapped at her. Then, looking at Beth, I asked, 'Did Harry Trent or Ted Kirby stand you up on your date, Beth?'

She didn't answer for a moment. She just gaped at me as if I was crazy. 'No, neither,' she said. 'It was another boy. But — but why do you ask, Gerry?'

'Maybe I just like to ask questions of people,' I grunted, and picked up my hat. 'Let's go.'

I closed up shop, rang for the night elevator, and the three of us rode it down to the lobby. We went out onto the street, and were in luck. A cab was parked at the curb. I whistled, and it rolled down to a stop. I helped Paula and Beth in, and started in myself. But I stopped. I did because a hand slid over my shoulder and took away my gun *again*. And another hand shoved the muzzle of another gun into the small of my back!

22

'Get in, Barnes! Let's not keep the ladies waiting. In!'

Rat Eyes Kirby emphasized the last with a violent shove that sent me sprawling flat on the cab floor.

'Don't!' he bit off as both Paula and Beth evidently started to yell.

Then he slid in himself, jammed the jump seat down on my legs, and sat on it. But not too heavily. By then the cab was in motion, and in an abstract sort of way I wondered if Jake or Mike was driving. I couldn't see. I couldn't see a darn thing. And it took a few seconds for the reason to sink into my throbbing head. The cab's windows were blacked out all around. Curtains, or what, I didn't know or care. Both my legs from the knee down were going numb because of the pressing brace of the jump seat stopping circulation. My hands were caught under me, and when I tried to pull them out something blocked both elbows. Kirby felt, or sensed, the movement, and pressed down harder on the seat.

'Relax, Barnes,' he said in a pleasant voice. 'Nobody wants to hurt you. And you won't be there long, anyway. Here. A little better?'

He eased off some of the jump seat pressure on my legs, and it was much better.

'What's the idea?' was the only bright question I could think up.

'Just a little conference,' Kirby told me smoothly. 'A couple of things have come up. You'll know all about it soon, so be quiet. You too, ladies. This thing wouldn't be heard. Besides, I don't like killing women as a rule.'

'So gallant of you!' I heard Paula say in an icy voice.

Kirby chuckled, and then Beth Price spoke in a tone that was a cross between a hoarse whisper and somebody tearing a strip of cloth. 'What is the meaning of this, Ted? I . . . I don't understand!'

'You soon will, baby,' he told her. 'Right now, enjoy the ride.'

That ended the conversation. I didn't mind, exactly. I was content, if you could call it such, with trying to beat off the numbing ache crawling up my body, and trying to figure by the turns made in what direction the cab was traveling. And then suddenly we made a sharp turn, slowly rolled forward down a slight incline, and then came to a full stop. I heard doors shut just as the cab stopped, and a second later there was light as the door at my feet end was opened by Kirby. Almost instantly, the weight was removed from my legs.

'Stay put a minute, Barnes,' Kirby said. And he tapped my foot with his gun. 'All right, ladies, out!'

Paula and Beth stepped out, careful not to step on me. Then Rat Eyes Kirby grabbed my feet and pulled. I slid halfway out on my face and belly before he let my feet drop. Struggling against the dancing lights in my head, and the weird roaring in my ears, I slowly pushed myself the rest of the way out of the cab and up onto my feet. Then, as the threatening blackout haze faded in my brain, I forced myself to look around.

We were in the same basement garage Jake had shanghaied me to the day before. And to practically make it like old home week, the ape himself climbed out from behind the cab's wheel and grinned at me like he thought I was the funniest thing he'd ever seen in his life.

'Maybe we should keep this guy's gun,' he chuckled at Kirby. 'Don't seem like he's ever going to get a chance to use it, huh?'

'No, but some guys just never learn,' Kirby added his own chuckle. Then, with a wave of his gun that included the three of us, he said, 'Over there, and inside.'

As we were headed toward the elevator, I took a quick look at Paula and Beth. Paula's face showed cool defiance that belied the raging fire of anger that flamed underneath. Beth's face was more of a puzzle. I couldn't tell whether she was getting a bobby-sock kick out of it all, or was about ready to fall over in a dead faint. When we were in the elevator, I tried to touch Paula's hand, but Kirby was between us so I had to give it up.

At the end of our ride aloft came another surprise. When Kirby and Jake herded us out of the car and into the half-moon-shaped room I had seen once before, the first thing I saw was Mike standing guard over Rita Rollins and Harry Trent. At the sight of us, Rita's whole face lighted up with joy and relief. Exactly opposite, Trent's face went dark with anger. He even started out of his chair as though to come for me, but Mike's ham hand slapped him right back into it.

'Barnes, I'll — '

But that was all Trent was able to choke out. Mike calmly slapped the rest back down his throat.

'Just take it easy, all of you!' Kirby suddenly spoke up. 'Just don't talk. You'll all have plenty of chance to talk soon.'

And with a faint movement of his head toward Jake and Mike that meant for us to do just that, or else, Kirby went over to the desk and picked up the bush-o-phone. A couple of movements later, he put it down and jabbed one of the desk buttons. We all heard the click of the center door latch.

'This way,' Kirby told us, and motioned. 'Mr. White will see you right away.'

'The *hell* he'll see me!' Trent shouted wildly. 'I *demand* — '

The guy just couldn't seem to refrain from begging for it. And he got it. A cuff on the head from Mike that spilled him out of the chair. And a one-handed yank from Mike that brought him up on his feet. And lastly a shove that sent him through the door Kirby had pushed open. I brought up the rear, with the exception of Kirby and Jake. As a result, I heard Kirby tell Mike to go down below and take the cab away and get rid of it. And somehow it made me feel a little better to hear that. One less of the enemy around was something, anyway . . . I hoped!

White was seated over at his desk. He was suave, polished, and so gracious. He bowed, though, without getting up.

'Good evening, ladies,' he said. 'Lieutenant Trent, and, of course, Mr. Barnes. Please, will you?'

The last was accompanied by a sweep

of his hand that included five chairs arranged semicircle in front of his desk. I moved quickly and sat down in the middle one, directly facing him. Paula sat down at my right; and Rita, after a moment's hesitation, sat down on her right. Beth Price, trembling visibly, practically collapsed in the chair to my left. But Harry Trent refused to sit down. He gripped the back of the remaining chair and glared daggers at White.

'I demand an explanation right now!' he shouted. 'I'm an officer in the U. S. navy, and by God I won't stand for this sort of thing. I'll — '

Jake moved like a cat toward Trent, and the U. S. navy officer shut up. A quick motion from White, however, ordered Jake to keep his hands to himself. Then White smiled pleasantly at Trent, but just with his lips.

'It's an interesting point of law, Lieutenant,' he said softly. 'Is an officer on terminal leave technically a civilian, or not? I mean, would he be tried for murder, perhaps a double murder, by a naval court or a civilian court? What would you say, sir?'

Trent didn't say anything. His face went all colors, and ended up white as a sheet. For a couple of seconds he hung onto the chair to steady himself, and then he stumbled around it and sat down.

'I — I didn't murder anybody!' he said hoarsely.

'Then you *probably* have nothing to fear,' White said smoothly. And then the smile and the damn pink-tinted eyes were directed at me. 'Haven't you any questions, Mr. Barnes? After all, I *was* sincere about my offer.'

I studied his pink eyes for a moment, and let him wait some more while I slid my hands down my legs to my knees and leaned forward on them.

'No, I haven't any questions, White,' I said. 'Your latest move fooled me, though. Having them all drop into my office. I guessed that you were needling me into action.'

'Perhaps I owe you an apology, sir.' He smiled. 'I really intended to leave you alone to your own methods. However, on thinking it over I thought of a plan that would save me time. And possibly money.'

White stopped himself and gave a little half shake of his head.

'But maybe I won't save money,' he said, still looking at me. 'Mr. Barnes, if you can give me the map, or tell me where it is, I'll still gladly pay you the one hundred thousand dollars!'

I heard Beth gasp at my left, but it was quickly drowned out by Paula's sharp question.

'What map?'

'Please, Miss Grant!' White said, slowly moving his eyes from my face to hers. 'Such a silly question! Now, ladies and gentlemen,' White went on like a judge from the bench, 'we're gathered here to obtain a certain map. One of you has it in your possession. Or knows where it can be found. Believe me, I don't like violence in any form, and so I make this offer to each of you. Produce that map for me and I'll pay one hundred thousand dollars, cash! Also, no questions asked. The matter will end right there for both of us. Well?'

I heard Beth Price gasp again, and sort of lean forward as if to say something. Almost instantly, though, she sat back again. Her funny action meant I was unable to take a look at any of the others to see how they were taking the tempting offer.

Well, for about a minute nobody said a word. Then White sighed and shook his head sadly. 'I'm sorry,' he said, 'but perhaps I was counting too much on your individual intelligence. And so I'm forced to pursue the only alternative course. That is, to force you one by one to tell the truth. This gentleman, Jake, will . . . assist you. Believe me, he's expert — not to say unique — in his methods of persuasion.'

'You wouldn't dare!' Paula suddenly burst out in withering scorn.

'But I *would*, Miss Grant!' White corrected her. 'With an estimated ten million dollars in gold involved, I would dare a whole lot of things. And I think I know what's in back of your words. In that, too, you're also wrong. None of you knows exactly where you are. That is, with the exception of Mr. Barnes, who perhaps knows the general locality. I'll let Mr. Barnes worry about that, however.'

White glanced at me with a smile. And I didn't need even one guess to get what he meant by the crack.

'No, Miss Grant,' he said, looking back to Paula again. 'You all were brought here with certain precautions on our part. Those who leave . . . will leave the same way. However, I'm a fair man, I think. I appeal again to one of you. Which one, I don't know at this moment. However, when Jake takes you into the next room, tell him what you want to tell me. I give you my word that none of the others will know it was you . . . who was the sensible, and *lucky* one!'

Pink Eyes White paused for emphasis, or lack of breath, or maybe both. Then, after sweeping us all with his eyes, he finally centered his gaze on Paula. Ice coated my heart, to be melted away by seething fury almost instantly. This was *it* . . . coming up!

'You dare me, Miss Grant, so Jake will talk with you first! Jake!'

Jake, a half kid-like, half wolf-like smile

on his big face, stepped around in front of Trent and moved toward Paula. He held a gun in his hands, and for a second his eyes flickered my way.

The instant they moved away from me, I dropped my hands off my knees and made as though I was going to lunge from my chair. Jake halted and half-spun, his gun coming up. So I shot him right in the belly, but I didn't watch him fall down like two tons of brick. I saw Kirby take a half-step forward and whip up his hand. I lunged to the right, spilling Paula off her chair, and fired my gun again at the same time. I heard Kirby's bullet whisper, but I saw the small blue hole that suddenly appeared square in the middle of Kirby's forehead.

In that instant, somebody screamed with rage. It was White, and his hand was coming up over the edge of his desk with a gun in it when I fired my third shot. As I pulled the trigger, he had two pink-tinted eyes, but right after my gun made sound he had one pink-tinted eye, and one that was a gory hole in his head that dripped blood down his cheek as he slumped forward over the desk.

My gun? Well, I can be kicked by a mule just so often before I do something about it. And I had. In my apartment, before I went to the office to meet Rita, I had clipped a Luger twenty-five to my right leg, just up under the pants cuff. Yes, the mate to the one I had given as a souvenir to Paula. And so when Kirby took my shoulder-holstered gun from me as he had once before, and Jake once, too, he thought I would be a harmless fellow from then on.

Anyway, just as soon as White started on the journey to wherever people like him go, I got out of my chair fast and beat Trent to it by a nice margin. I mean, in picking up the gun in Jake's limp fingers. The ape wasn't dead, yet, but he soon would be. And without commenting on Trent's snarl of disappointment, I quickly went over and picked up Kirby's gun. Then around the desk to collect the third one in White's stiffening fingers.

Outside of Trent's snarl, no one had made a sound. Nor did they make a sound as curiosity got the best of me, and

I reached down and jerked away the robe over White's lap. I was wrong. It must have been my imagination taking me for a sleigh ride. I couldn't possibly have seen White peeking at me through the potted plants in the Biltmore cocktail lounge. His left leg was completely withered from the hip down.

Before straightening up, a thought suddenly occurred to me. Without them knowing it, I took a good sneak look at Paula, Rita, Beth and Trent. And if I had had any doubts, they all vanished right then and there. Three pairs of eyes watched me. The fourth pair was riveted to the top of White's head on the desk blotter, and held an expression that I could read like words in a books. Then the tension in the room snapped as Beth Price started crying like crazy. Paula, still half-crouched on the floor where I had shoved her, started to get up and comfort her. I moved even faster, and used a more effective method. I slapped Beth hard, and the wailing died cold. Paula's eyes blazed.

'Did you *have* to do that?' she snapped.

'Yes, and it worked!' I snapped back. 'Now pull yourselves together, all of you. We're getting out of this place fast, before that other ape gets back.'

'Damn right!' Trent said hotly. And then quickly grinned at me. 'Good shooting, Barnes,' he said.

'I've had a lot of practice here and there,' I shrugged it off. Then, 'Okay, let's go. Wait, let me try that door first.'

As I said those words, I walked quickly over to it, eased it open, and poked my head and my gun outside. The half-moon-shaped room was empty. I opened the door wide and stepped back.

'Go ahead, Paula, the rest of you,' I said.

Paula led the way, and when they were all out I took the three guns I had collected out of my pocket and tossed them back into the room. As I did, my eyes met Jake's. His were in the last glassy stage. Using up his last breath, he spoke. 'Nutty as a fruit cake! I shoulda remem . . . ' And he died.

I closed the door and went over to the single elevator, and jabbed the button. I put my gun in my pocket and just stood there ignoring the others while the car came up. When it did, and the door slid open and I didn't see Mike inside, I took my hand off the gun in my pocket.

'Get in,' I grunted, and led the way.

When they were all in, I pushed the button, but not the one I'd seen Jake push the day before. The one above it for the lobby floor of the building.

'Just walk along with me,' I said as the car started down. 'We're leaving here by the lobby. If anybody's in it, just keep walking. Understand?'

There was a collection of grunts in reply, and Paula's shaky whisper in my ear.

'My hero, I think you're pretty swell!'

I grinned, because that made me feel pretty good. Then the dropping car eased to a stop, and the automatic doors slid open. It was the building lobby, and we were all in luck. Nobody there but us. We walked through it and out the double doors that brought us out onto Riverside Drive. And we had no sooner come to a stop on the sidewalk than Rita grabbed my left arm and let out a yell.

'*Gerry*, the rat's running away! Stop him! Shoot him!'

The 'rat' was Trent, and he certainly was making tracks and distance. Even if I had jerked my gun out, I wouldn't have been able to pull the trigger before he was around the corner and out of sight. So instead, I smothered a curse, and shook off Rita's arm with a shrug.

'Don't worry,' I said. 'This town is full of cops. What we want right now is a — '

I didn't finish, because at that moment an empty cab came cruising by and swung quickly into the curb at my whistle. When it did, the three women just stood there looking at me. Shock still held them more or less tongue-tied, but reaction was setting in fast. Particularly with Beth Price. Her face was like nervous jelly. I made a quick decision.

'You put Beth up for the night, Paula,' I said, and motioned them into the cab. 'Your place is nearest, so we'll go there first.'

Paula started to say something, but I had already turned to give the cabby the address. When I got in and took one of the jump seats, she seemed to have changed her mind. We rode to Paula's apartment building in strained silence.

'I don't think a drink would hurt anybody,' Paula broke the silence when the cab pulled up.

I shook my head, opened the door, and told the cabby to keep his flag down. 'No,' I said. 'I have a date with Bierman. You and Beth go on up, and stay there. I'll drop Rita off at her place, and probably phone you later.'

The helping hand I had extended helped Beth, but Paula brushed right by it.

'A date, of course!' she said icily. 'Thank you for such an interesting evening!'

I clenched my teeth and let her go. When I got back in the cab and gave the driver Rita's address, she snuggled over close with a little contented, and sort of triumphant, sigh. I sat still.

23

When I paid off the cabby in front of Rita's place, her face lighted up with pleasure and she giggled like a new bride.

'So you do want a drink, don't you, darling?' she purred, and clung to my arm as the cab rolled off.

'Yeah, I think we could both do with one,' I grunted, and walked her up the steps.

She let us in and in silence we went up the three flights. She went first into her apartment and switched on the lights. My glance around showed that it was pretty well straightened up; not a bit like the last time I'd seen it. I pushed the doors shut and took off my hat. Rita turned with a smile, and then something changed the smile to a faint frown.

'Over there,' she said, and pointed at the liquor cabinet. 'Make them triple strength. But I must look like a hag. Ten seconds, Gerry.'

I watched her go slowly into her bedroom. Then I walked over to the liquor cabinet and poured myself three fingers, and downed it. Then I made two, but not triple strength, and took them over to the coffee table. I dropped myself on one end of the couch and stared unseeingly at the two drinks. I was dead for sleep, and I ached all over. But that wasn't it, exactly. Truthfully, I hurt like hell in body, mind and soul.

It wasn't ten seconds, it was several minutes before Rita came out of her bedroom. She was wearing a brilliant little hostess gown number intended to blind the strongest pair of eyes at ten yards. Surprisingly, though, she didn't try to sit skin to skin with me as of yore. Instead, she regarded me gravely, then picked up her drink and sat down at the far end of the couch. The first pull she took of it could have floated a canoe. I took a deep breath and looked at her.

'Just one, so make it last,' I said in a voice I hardly recognized as my own. 'When we're through, you're going to change back and put a few things in a bag.'

Her face lighted up, and then in a flash her expression changed to that of a kid who had hoped so hard Santa Claus would bring her *the* doll, and had lost.

'Oh,' she said softly. Then, 'What do you mean, Gerry?'

I didn't look at her. I reached for my drink. 'You and I are keeping my date with Bierman together, Rita,' I said.

A moment of silence. 'What about Trent, Gerry? He — '

'I'm not interested in Trent,' I said, still not looking at her. 'If Bierman wants to be, that's his business.'

Another moment of silence was too much for me. My guts were tied in aching knots. I wanted to hit something; like a stone wall.

'You little fool!' I blazed, facing her. 'Money, money! Always *money*!'

'Damn right!' she blazed back at me. 'If you'd lived the childhood I — '

'Oh, skip it!' I cut her off savagely. 'You wore that record out two years ago. My God, Rita, how . . . how in hell did you think you could get away with it? *Two murders!*'

'*One!*' she flung at me. 'Just Mather. And I'll plead self-defense. That guy was a leech, a bum . . . Gerry, Trent killed Jord Akerson. I can prove it.'

'You can't,' I said. 'You can't, because you killed Akerson, too!'

I thought she was going to come for me, but she didn't. Instead the anger faded and a coy cunning seeped into her eyes. 'Nuts!' she said. 'Trent killed Jord Akerson. He was jealous. They had a fight right here in this apartment the day before yesterday. Trent said he'd kill Jord, and — '

'Nuts, also!' I stopped her. And everything in the whole world seemed flat and stinko. 'Trent wasn't in New York the day before yesterday. He was in Washington. That can be proved. For Christ's sake, stop lying! You think I'm happy?'

She didn't reply to that. She didn't say anything until she'd finished her drink. Then it was to ask me for another. I started to shake my head, but what the hell. I got up and mixed her another one.

'All right, lies are out,' she said slowly when that one was half-gone. 'It was self-defense both times. I swear it! I . . . Gerry, isn't it funny?'

'What?' I said.

'In the taxi coming down from Paula's,' she said, 'I could suddenly tell that you were the best detective in the world. That . . . that you suddenly knew everything. Oh, of course I hoped and prayed that maybe . . . Darling, you're so clever. And I do love you so. I always have, no matter what you think.'

I didn't say anything, and I didn't think anything, either. The brain was too much of an aching void to even begin. I just hated Rita's guts. And my own for what I had to do.

'What did I do wrong, Gerry?'

Her question hauled me up from down under.

'Killed two guys,' I mumbled.

'But it was self-defense! And, and the whole world should be glad those two lechers are gone.'

'Maybe,' I said. Then, with an angry

gesture, 'Finish that drink, and get dressed.'

'No, not yet!' she snapped. 'I want to know how you figured it out. And, Gerry . . . you could be wrong, you know.'

I started to say that I'd wait and let Bierman listen in, but something in her eyes stopped me. Maybe it started me wondering if I was wrong . . . and praying that I was.

'All right!' I snapped back at her, and took such a savage pull of my drink that I nearly gagged. 'First, Akerson. Yesterday, when you, and Beth, and Trent, and Mather plowed into Paula's apartment. You started to go to her bedroom for the habitual primping, but you didn't. Because you knew Akerson was in there dead. Or had been in there dead, the last time you saw him. The reason you dropped in with the gang was because you were nuts to find out whether or not he had been found, wasn't it?'

She didn't say anything. And didn't have to as far as I was concerned.

'This morning in my office,' I went on, 'you asked me if I thought Trent had knifed the guy in the throat in Paula's bedroom. There was not a line printed *how* Akerson died until this afternoon's late editions. Nor in what *room* of Paula's he had been murdered. And don't tell me that Trent told you last night after his visit to the morgue. He couldn't have found *that* out down there.'

'Anything else, lover?' Rita asked, and actually smiled.

'A few things,' I said. 'In the Biltmore with Paula and Beth and me this afternoon. You asked a couple of times who had been killed. And then let it go because, of course, you knew. And before joining us you overheard our talk about Mather having a key to Paula's apartment.'

The way she laughed at that made little shivers streak up and down my spine.

'You're wonderful, darling!' she cried. 'And crazy!'

I should have got mad, but I didn't. I guess I was beyond getting sore, or real mad, or anything.

Her lips were parted in a smile and her eyes were bright. But the rest of her face was starting to sag. Holding her smile, she put down her glass and then cross-rested her hands at the base of her throat.

'Anything else?' she asked brightly. 'Or is that supposed to be enough?'

'Did you see Trent today, save for tonight?' I asked.

'No!' The answer came fast.

'But you did see Mather twice,' I said. 'Once this morning when he got you away from here so's Trent could hunt for the gold map. And this afternoon when you met him coming here to see me, and you went to his apartment where you shot him.'

She laughed that way again, and I was almost tempted to stop right there and take her down to Bierman's office where we could finish it.

'I saw Mather this morning, yes.' She nodded. Then suddenly her eyes went wide. 'Then it *was* Trent who came in here and wrecked the place? Not one of White's men?'

'It was, and had to be,' I told her. 'It wasn't one of White's men because White wanted to see me. Kirby would have carted me off in Mike's car outside, and not waited to force me with a gun in his pocket later. Mather was with you. So it was Trent. He knew you had killed Akerson and taken the wallet with the map in it.'

'Oh, did he?' she sneered. 'Who told him, may I ask?'

'Mather,' I said, and watched her face. 'Mather went to Paula's yesterday morning to show her his new car. He didn't see Paula, but he did see somebody else. You. Maybe with Akerson, or maybe leaving Paula's alone. Mather can't tell us now. But this morning when he went to Trent to make contact again with Akerson, Trent told him what had happened to Akerson. And so Mather added two and two. He told you the correct score this afternoon in his apartment, and made a proposition, didn't he?'

'Did he?' she came right back, but the spirit had gone from her voice.

'Yes,' I said bluntly. 'He had figured by then that you had killed Akerson and had the map. So, if you dealt in with him he would just forget where he'd seen you yesterday morning. Maybe he made passes, or maybe be tried a grab for your purse, thinking the map was in it. So you shot him.'

I paused for a moment and leaned a little toward her.

'So you shot him with the Luger twenty-five you'd found in Paula's bottom bureau drawer when you opened it to get something to wipe your fingerprints from that knife. The Luger that was in your purse when you dropped it in my office early this afternoon. And picked it up before I could, with that crack about compacts and stuff being heavy these days. Right?'

'Wrong, lover,' she said with a stiff smile. 'Who says I was in Mather's apartment this afternoon? This morning, yes, but — '

'I do!' I cut her off. 'Tonight in my office you asked me if Mather had told me all the things I knew in Trent's apartment this morning. Rita . . . I didn't tell you that Mather was there when I was. So it was Mather who told you that the three of us were there!'

I paused to give her a chance to say something. She didn't say a word. She just sat there hands crossed below her throat, and her whole face slowly giving way to the fierce emotions raging within.

'You insane, crazy little fool you!' I had to say, or else hit her. 'Tonight, when I shot White, only you looked sorry, and sore. The big money ... shot right between your fingers. And with the money lost you began to get scared. You wanted me to shoot Trent, when that yellow belly ran away from us. With Trent dead, too ...'

I choked on the rest, and let it slide. My head was beginning to hum. And I felt as though every drop of blood in me was draining out through my toes.

'Just why did you kill Akerson, Rita?' I asked. And, so help me, I prayed she'd give me an answer that really would put a jury on her side. 'Why *did* you?'

Her voice was like nobody's I had never heard before in my life. Dead flat. Completely drained of emotion.

'Who says I did? I was kidding when I said so.'

'I'm saying it,' I replied quietly. 'Maybe my case isn't airtight, Rita, but it doesn't have to be. I don't work by the rules of the book . . . but Lieutenant Bierman does. Maybe he's figured it all out by now, himself. I don't know. But, Rita, what I know added to whatever Bierman knows! Don't you see that . . . Why in hell *did* you kill him? Was he sore because you collected the money White sent to General Delivery for him, and kept it?'

She came out of her trance, and sat up straight with a gasp. 'So you know that, too?'

I nodded, but it had actually been some adding of two and two on my own part. Rita had taken White's phone call at the Club Royale at the exact time Akerson had stated in his letter to White via Trent and Mather. So she had collected the money letter because either she or Akerson was smart. And Jake was dumb because he expected a man, and paid no attention to women asking for mail.

'Yes, and lots of things I haven't even mentioned,' I said aloud. 'But there's a couple of things I don't know. How and why did you go into Paula's apartment? Had you got her key from Mather?'

She didn't answer for a moment, and when she looked at me I was sure she was going to fight it out . . . hopelessly. But I was wrong. A weird, almost eerie change came over her face. It was sort of part heartbreak and part the kind of relief that can be felt only in the soul. And the words she spoke surprised me more than any others I had heard for a long, long time.

'I didn't use any key, Gerry. Paula's apartment door wasn't locked. It was actually open an inch. I guess the latch hadn't caught when she'd gone out.'

She stopped, but I could only look at her, pop-eyed. So the most baffling thing of the whole crazy case actually hadn't even existed!

'But — but *why* Paula's place?' I eventually heard my far-off voice say.

'Jord and I had had a fight the night before,' Rita started talking in a dull voice. 'It wasn't over anything important. Jord just got drunk . . . and nasty. He left saying I could go to hell. That Trent was coming back from Washington the next day, and that the two of them would complete the deal. And I'd be out. Well, yesterday morning I went to see Trent. To tell him if I didn't get my share, I'd raise hell. After all, it was legally Philippine government gold and stuff. I could go to some official, or somebody.'

I thought of those poor dead guys in that submarine, and felt sick with shame. I didn't say anything to Rita. I just waited for her to get her breath.

'Well, I met Jord downstairs,' she went on. 'He must have spent the rest of the night getting more slopped. He didn't seem to remember our fight. I . . . Well, I thought it best to keep him away from Trent. I remembered Paula had an apartment in the same building. I decided we'd both go up there and get a drink. A couple of more and Jord would pass out. When I'd sobered him up at my place we could talk sense. Anyway, I didn't want him to see Trent until I was sure he wasn't really sore at me.'

She paused again, and so I said a few words. 'Paula wasn't home, but her door was open. So you and Akerson went in for the drink, anyway?'

'That's right,' she said without looking at me. Then, with a low moan and a shudder, she went on, 'But Jord didn't want a drink. He saw that knife on Paula's desk. He'd got one, too. He . . . Gerry, if you ever did have a kind thought for me, believe me now. He went suddenly insane! Said all kinds of crazy things. I damn near died of fright. I couldn't get past him out the door, so I ran into the bedroom. He ran after me . . . laughing crazy like, and saying he was only kidding. But he grabbed me, and . . . and somehow the knife went into his throat.'

The last was a whisper that I almost didn't catch. She went on whispering, but a little louder.

'When he fell back on the bed his jacket opened. I saw his wallet. He had taken the map out of it the time he showed it to me. Gerry . . . all that money! And . . . and I really had only killed him by accident. Gerry, darling, I can't even tell you what came into my mind. I only know I took the wallet, and the map was there. I thought of fingerprints and pulled open that drawer. I saw the Luger and took it. I don't know why. Maybe I thought I'd have to protect myself later, or something. I . . . '

Her voice stumbled to silence that lasted several seconds.

'The rest you know,' she said. 'This morning I thought you had wrecked this place. That you knew something already. I knew you hadn't found the map, because I had it with me. So I put that stuff in that envelope and gave it to you. If you wondered about me I knew that you'd open it and look. Mather? Yes, Gerry. He did see me leaving Paula's. And he made me a proposition like you said. And got rough. God, how I hate men who paw! I — I didn't mean to shoot him. It — it just happened. Honest to God, Gerry, I didn't mean to kill either of them! It was just . . . '

She stopped and worked her mouth silently. I said nothing.

'Gerry, you understand, don't you? Do you suppose . . . I mean . . . well, if there were all men on the jury. Do you think . . . ?'

I gave her my honest opinion with a shake of my head.

'Where's the map, Rita?' I asked a moment later.

'In the mail, Gerry. In an envelope I addressed to your office, and dropped in the mail chute after I left you tonight. You see, Gerry, when you told me you had been offered a hundred thousand by White, I thought maybe that you would . . . Well, that is . . . Oh!'

The last was because she'd read my thoughts through my eyes, and knew what I thought of her for even thinking what she had thought I might do. And then her hand slipped down between the V of her hostess gown and came up with Paula's little Luger. Yes, I'd known it was there. I'd noticed that the faint outline of it made one curve too many. But I hadn't expected it that soon. Yet somehow I wasn't surprised . . . or even alarmed. Anyway, I didn't move a muscle.

'One more won't help you any,' I said, flat-voiced.

She looked at me, startled, and began to cry softly.

'Oh, Gerry darling, *no*! I . . . Why did it *have* to be Paula? Why did you *have* to meet her? We were having such fun. Everything was so swell. I wonder . . . I wonder if you hadn't met her, if we . . . you and I . . . mightn't have . . . ?'

She said more, but I wasn't listening. I didn't care a damn what she was saying. I didn't care a damn about anything. Maybe I was crying a little myself in my heart. I don't know. Rita Rollins, the peppy bundle of tricks that I once . . . I just didn't care. And then suddenly it was too late.

She put the Luger to her temple and pulled the trigger!

24

Well, it's now a little over twenty hours since Rita pulled the trigger of that Luger, but the echo of the shot is as clear in my head as though I'd just heard it. And so is the echo of Lieutenant Frank Bierman's blistering, blasting words that poured into my ears by the hour. Half a dozen times last night and today I told him the whole story in minute detail. And each time his blood pressure went even higher. He cussed at me, cussed me out, and damn near cussed me under. I did this wrong. I did that wrong. In fact, I did everything wrong, save one small item. I did crack the case. That, friend Bierman just couldn't boot out the window. And so in the end — about two hours ago — he did send me home with a gold star for final results, if for nothing else.

Yes, the map was in my mail this morning. And by now it is in the hands of certain parties in Washington who know exactly what to do with it. Who knows, maybe one day soon I'll get an official letter I'll be proud to show my grandchildren . . . if the Gerry twig of the Barnes family tree ever grows that big.

And White's twenty-five thousand? I picked that up at the Biltmore this morning, and put it in another envelope addressed to the New York headquarters of the Fight Cancer Fund. Nick took it around there for me. And whether it's tainted money or not, which I don't know, it will at least be used to fight a national battle in its way as grim and fearful as the recent one we fought against the Nazis and the Japs.

And White himself? All Bierman had unearthed since the last time he opened the sluice gates of his vocal wrath upon me was that White was a Mr. T. T. White who had been living on the whole top floor of a certain Riverside Drive address for two years. That he was a cripple and apparently wealthy. That he had all kinds of visitors — some nice-looking and some not so nice. Bierman thinks he can tie a few unsolved fraud and robbery cases to

White. And if so, more power to him. As for me, the hell with White. I'm not interested a rap in the *why* or *how* of him before my bullet smacked through his eye.

Nor *what*, if anything, Bierman decides to do about Trent.

Mike, incidentally, has not been picked up yet. But he will be soon, because like Jake, he is the type to run his big feet right over the cliff eventually.

And so ends my first case. And here I sit in my place thinking about it. Or, rather, trying not to think about it as I wait for Paula to show up. She insisted on coming over to play nurse for me, and I do feel like hell. Besides, she wants to pay the four cents balance I've got coming of her fee. I'll throw her out as soon as I can, because I do need bed awful bad. But I don't know as I will, at that. I mean, be able to. Paula mostly gets what Paula wants. And in my weakened condition . . .

Anyway, here I sit. And really thinking of Rita Rollins, if you must have the truth. I know, I should be thinking of Akerson, and Mather, and how Rita really was a . . . But I'm not. I'm thinking about what she said. About if Paula had never come into the picture. I wonder if Rita and I . . . ? Well, would marrying money have straightened her out and removed that crazy twist in her crazy head? I mean . . . Well, supposing Rita and I . . . ?

Oh-oh! Paula's at the door! Some other time about Rita. Right now I must find out just how weak a guy in my condition really is . . . or *is not*!

We do hope that you have enjoyed reading this large print book.

Did you know that all of our titles are available for purchase?

We publish a wide range of high quality large print books including:
Romances, Mysteries, Classics
General Fiction
Non Fiction and Westerns

Special interest titles available in large print are:
The Little Oxford Dictionary
Music Book, Song Book
Hymn Book, Service Book

Also available from us courtesy of Oxford University Press:
Young Readers' Dictionary
(large print edition)
Young Readers' Thesaurus
(large print edition)

For further information or a free brochure, please contact us at:
Ulverscroft Large Print Books Ltd.,
The Green, Bradgate Road, Anstey,
Leicester, LE7 7FU, England.
Tel: (00 44) 0116 236 4325
Fax: (00 44) 0116 234 0205

*Other titles in the
Linford Mystery Library:*

GHOST LAKE

V. J. Banis

Its real name is Caspar Lake, but people call it Ghost Lake. Years ago, a ferryboat went down in a storm, drowning everyone on board — and some say their souls have never rested . . . Beth Nolan travels to the nearby town at the invitation of an old school friend, but no sooner does she arrive than she is plunged into the murky depths of the brutal murder of a young woman. Beth must find answers — or risk joining the dead in the haunted depths of Ghost Lake . . .

THE EYE STONES

Harriet Esmond

A shock awaits Deborah Ritchie when she arrives to stay with her recently married sister. She is told that the couple have both perished tragically in a fire which destroyed their home. Alone in the bleak Norfolk brecklands, Deborah is forced to accept hospitality from the forbidding Sir Randall Gaunt. She gladly leaves Sir Randall and his grim anatomical practices for the warm companionship of young Lord Stannard and his family. But before long, she is inextricably involved in a nightmare of mystery and unimagined evil . . .

ANCIENT EVIL RETURNS

Richard A. Lupoff

A youthful journalist seeks to unravel the mysterious disaster that struck a New England town nearly a century ago . . . A young couple, stranded by a monstrous storm, seek shelter in a darkened town and discover a dangerous cult . . . A peculiar child is born . . . A young woman and her boyfriend find themselves in terrible danger . . . A brilliant academic begins to make a disquieting discovery . . . These are the problems faced by ordinary people as they encounter extraordinary mysteries when *Ancient Evil Returns*.